"What a way ...
David mana...
drawing a ragged breath

"Wh-what happened?" If anything Claudia was more disoriented than he was.

"I must have been half asleep," said David, as if to himself. "I woke up and there was someone there and suddenly... I'm sorry, I didn't realize it was you."

Claudia's legs trembled so violently when she tried to stand up that she had to hang on to the bed. Sitting on the edge of the bed, she peered at herself in the mirror and grimaced at her reflection as she remembered it was her thirtieth birthday. She was supposed to wake up this morning a changed woman, mature, confident, in control—not moaning with pleasure in the arms of a man who didn't even realize who she was!

Dear Reader,

Welcome to

Everyone has special occasions in their life—times of celebration and excitement. Maybe it's a romantic event, an engagement or a wedding—or perhaps a wonderful family occasion, such as the birth of a baby. Or even a personal milestone—a thirtieth or fortieth birthday!

These are all important times in our lives and in **The Big Event!** you can see how different couples react to these events. Whatever the occasion, romance and drama are guaranteed!

We'll be featuring one book each month from May to August in 1998, bringing you terrific stories from some of your favorite authors. And, to make this miniseries extraspecial, **The Big Event!** will also appear in the Harlequin Presents® series.

This month we're delighted to bring you Jessica Hart's bubbly romance, *Birthday Bride* and look out next month for *The Diamond Dad* by Lucy Gordon.

Happy reading!

The Editors

P.S. Follow the series into our Presents line in September with Kathryn Ross's *Bride for a Year*.

Birthday Bride
Jessica Hart

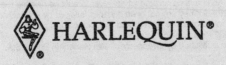

TORONTO • NEW YORK • LONDON
AMSTERDAM • PARIS • SYDNEY • HAMBURG
STOCKHOLM • ATHENS • TOKYO • MILAN • MADRID
PRAGUE • WARSAW • BUDAPEST • AUCKLAND

ISBN 0-373-03511-X

BIRTHDAY BRIDE

First North American Publication 1998.

Birthday Bride
Jessica Hart

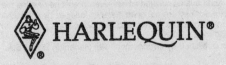

TORONTO • NEW YORK • LONDON
AMSTERDAM • PARIS • SYDNEY • HAMBURG
STOCKHOLM • ATHENS • TOKYO • MILAN • MADRID
PRAGUE • WARSAW • BUDAPEST • AUCKLAND

ISBN 0-373-03511-X

BIRTHDAY BRIDE

First North American Publication 1998.

Copyright © 1998 by Jessica Hart.

Birthday Bride
Jessica Hart

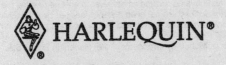

TORONTO · NEW YORK · LONDON
AMSTERDAM · PARIS · SYDNEY · HAMBURG
STOCKHOLM · ATHENS · TOKYO · MILAN · MADRID
PRAGUE · WARSAW · BUDAPEST · AUCKLAND

ISBN 0-373-03511-X

BIRTHDAY BRIDE

First North American Publication 1998.

CHAPTER ONE

IT WAS that girl again.

David's mouth turned disapprovingly down at the corners. He watched her hesitate, checking the seat number on her boarding card. She was tall and slender, with a swing of ash-blonde hair and an air of assurance that made her oblivious to the fact that she was blocking the aisle with that ridiculous bag of hers. He had thought her silly and superficial before, but now something about the way she stood there, holding up a patient queue, grated on David's nerves. There was an arrogance about her that reminded him all too bitterly of Alix.

She was pretty enough, David allowed grudgingly, if you liked that smart, superior look. Personally, he preferred girls with sweeter expressions and a more feminine wardrobe. This one was dressed with undeniable elegance in neutral colours—cool trousers, a silk top and a loose, unstructured jacket with the sleeves pushed casually up her arms. She would have looked much softer in a pretty dress, David thought, although, if she was anything like Alix, soft was the last word anyone should use to describe her.

Her eyes were moving slowly along the overhead lockers, studying the illuminated numbers, and David glanced at the empty seat beside him with a sudden sense of foreboding. He looked up just as her gaze dropped, and their eyes met with a jarring sense of recognition. With grim amusement, he saw that she was no more pleased to discover who she was to be sitting next to than he was.

Claudia was more than not pleased. She was dismayed. A frantic morning finishing off at work, a chaotic trip to the airport, a seven-hour flight from London and now she not only had to entrust her life to a plane that looked as if it was held together with sticky tape and bits of string, but she had to find herself sitting next to that supercilious, sarcastic man who had made her feel such a fool at Heathrow!

For one wild moment, Claudia considered asking the stewardess if she could change seats, but the rows behind looked pretty full, and there was an uncomfortably acute look in those cold grey eyes. She had a nasty feeling that he knew exactly what number was printed on her boarding card. If she made a fuss and insisted on moving, he would think that she was embarrassed to sit next to him, and Claudia had no intention of giving him the satisfaction of knowing that he had put her out of countenance.

Anyway, why should she let herself be intimidated by *him*? He was just some businessman, and a pretty charmless, humourless one at that. She would simply ignore him, she decided.

Hoisting her bag more firmly over her shoulder, Claudia stalked down the gangway. Sure enough, 12B was the empty seat beside him, but just as she prepared to settle down in haughty silence the man pulled out a report and ostentatiously buried his head in it. He could hardly have made it clearer that he didn't want to talk and was intent on ignoring *her*!

Claudia's lips thinned. There was something about this man that got under her skin. She had been the one who wanted to do the ignoring, but there was no point if he was just going to be grateful for her silence! No, it would be much more satisfying to see how far she could irritate him, and Claudia had only to look at the implacable set of his jaw to know that the best way to do *that* would be to make it impossible for him to ignore her as he was so intent on doing. After two and a half hours of conversation as inane and frivolous as she could make it, he would be regretting that he had ever opened his mouth at Heathrow!

The prospect was enough to curve Claudia's mouth into a satisfied smile. Perhaps she would enjoy this flight after all!

'Hello again!' she said brightly, and plumped herself down beside him.

Intensely suspicious of her smile, David gave a brusque nod and grunted some sort of greeting before pointedly turning his attention back to his report. Surely even she could take a hint like that?

Apparently not. 'It's quite a coincidence bumping into each other like this, isn't it?' she went on in the same chirpy voice, and David sighed inwardly. 'I didn't realise you were going to Telama'an as well.'

She bent forward to push her bag under the seat in front of her, and David was conscious of a subtle breath of fragrance as the blonde hair swung and shimmered distractingly at the edge of his vision.

'Why should you?' he said, trying to keep his eyes on the report and hoping that his repressive tone would be enough to make her realise that he was in no mood for conversation, but Claudia, delighted to see that his jaw was already tightening with irritation, refused to take the hint.

'I just assumed you would get off the plane in Dubai,' she said chattily. 'You know how it is when you speculate about your fellow travellers.'

'No,' said David, but she pretended that she hadn't heard.

'I just couldn't imagine you in a place like Shofrar,' she told him, settling herself back in her seat and slanting him a provocative look from under her lashes.

'Why ever not?' he said, goaded into a response just as he had decided to ignore her completely.

'Well, Shofrar sounds such an exciting place,' said Claudia, who was congratulating herself on her strategy. This was much more fun than sitting in frosty silence!

David scowled at her. 'Why don't you come right out and say that you think I look too boring to be going there?'

'Oh, but I don't mean that at *all*.' She pretended to flutter. She opened her eyes wide, and David, making the mistake of looking into them, was annoyed to notice that they were huge and extraordinarily beautiful, a smoky, smudgy colour somewhere between blue and grey.

'It's just that Shofrar sounds so wild and undeveloped and wonderfully *romantic*,' she was wittering on, and with something of an effort David dragged his gaze away. 'When I saw you at Heathrow, I thought you looked too conventional for the country.' Claudia put a hand to her mouth in mock dismay. 'Oh, dear, that sounds rude, doesn't it? I didn't mean it to be,' she lied. 'Steady and reliable are probably better words than conventional. You looked, you know, like the kind of man who would never give his wife any cause to worry and would always ring her if he was going to be late.'

David was unreasonably nettled by this tribute. Steadiness and reliability were qualities he had always valued, but this girl made them sound stolid and dull. She made *him* sound stolid and dull.

'I don't have a wife,' he said with something of a snap. 'And it may interest you to know that I have travelled extensively in Shofrar, and certainly more than you have if you think it is *wonderfully romantic*. It's a hard country,' he pointed out. 'It's hot and it's barren, with poor communications and no facilities for tourists. You're the one who's going to find herself out of place in Telama'an, not me. I may look conventional but I know the desert and I'm used to the conditions. You're too spoilt—oh, dear, that sounds rude, doesn't it?' He mimicked her tone with uncomfortable accuracy. 'I meant spoilt by luxurious living, that's all. I think you're going to find Telama'an something of a shock.'

'Really?' It was Claudia's turn to eye him frostily. 'And what makes you think that I haven't been to Telama'an before?'

'I've seen what you carry around in that bag of yours,' said David, nodding his head down at the shoulder bag that was squeezed under the seat in front of her. 'Nobody who had been anywhere near a desert would dream of packing a fraction of all that junk!'

Claudia bit her lip. She was beginning to wish that she hadn't tried to provoke him. Why couldn't he have been a decent, tactful, chivalrous type of man who wouldn't dream of mentioning that embarrassing incident at Heathrow?

She had been sitting opposite him in the departure lounge as they waited by the gate. There had been some delay in boarding, and the other passengers were milling around in frustration. Babies had cried, children had squabbled, ground staff had muttered into their walkie-talkies, but the man opposite her had just sat reading through papers with a stillness and concentration that completely ignored the hubbub around him.

He had rather ordinary brown hair and one of those austere faces that didn't give anything away, but Claudia, fascinated by his air of cool self-containment, had noticed a decidedly stubborn set to his jaw and an inflexible look about his mouth. She was secretly ashamed of the fact that the take-off always made her rather nervous, thinking that she ought by the age of twenty-nine to be blasé about jumping on and off planes, and although she was doing her best to seem cool and unconcerned she had found it oddly reassuring to watch the man working so quietly and competently in the midst of such chaos.

What would it be like to be that calm? Claudia was used to the frenetic activity of a television production company, and she thrived on panic and pressure. This man didn't look as if he knew the meaning of panic. He would probably be hell to work with, she'd decided. Efficient, yes, but deadly boring.

For some reason, Claudia's eyes had strayed back to his mouth. Well, maybe not exactly *boring*, she amended reluctantly. No one with a mouth like that could be really boring. It looked cool and firm, almost stern, but with an intriguing lift at the corners that made her wonder what he would look like if he smiled...

It was then that he had looked up, and Claudia had found herself staring into a pair of wintry grey eyes whose expression had sent the colour surging up her cheeks. Too late, she'd realised that she had been staring at him. He'd leant forward.

'Is something the matter?' he asked with careful restraint.

'No,' she said.

'My hair hasn't turned blue? There isn't any smoke coming out of my ears?'

Claudia pretended to check. 'No.'

'Then perhaps you could tell me what it is about me that has been fascinating you so much for the last twenty minutes?'

The withering tone deepened the flush in Claudia's cheeks. 'Nothing! I'm not the slightest bit interested in you! I was just...thinking.' Even to her own ears she sounded sullen and defensive.

'In that case, could you please think by staring at someone else? I'm trying to work, and it's not easy to concentrate with two great eyes boring into me.'

Claudia was amazed to discover that he had even noticed. So much for his powers of concentration! 'Certainly,' she said huffily, and got to her feet. 'I had no idea that sitting quietly minding my own business would be so disturbing! I'll go and stand in a corner and close my eyes, shall I? Or will my breathing be too distracting for you?'

The man looked profoundly irritated. 'I don't care what you do or where you do it, as long as you stop looking at me as if you're deciding whether to have me for lunch or not.'

'Lunch?' Claudia attempted a scornful laugh. 'I'm afraid my tastes run to something a little more substantial! You might do for a mid-morning snack, or perhaps a little something to have with a cup of tea!'

If she had hoped to rile him, she failed dismally. He looked at her incredulously for a moment, then shook his head as if deciding that she was too stupid to bother with any further, and returned his attention to his papers. Claudia felt about two inches high.

Furious, she made to stalk off in high dudgeon, but the bag she hoisted onto her shoulder was so overloaded that the strap snapped under the strain, and, to her horror, it crashed to the ground right at the man's feet.

She wouldn't have minded if he had jumped. She wouldn't have minded if he had clicked his tongue or looked startled or shown *some* kind of reaction, but he didn't even look up. Instead, he looked at the bag for about five seconds without saying anything, and then carried on reading. He could hardly have made it clearer that he thought she was too tedious and silly to merit any attention at all.

What if he thought she was deliberately trying to get him to notice her? The idea galvanised Claudia into action, and she dived to pick up the bag by its broken strap. It had landed on its bottom, which was fortunate, but that was where her luck ended. She hadn't realised that the zip was open, and as she grabbed the strap at one end the whole bag tilted, upturned, and the contents that she had shoved in frantically while the taxi waited to take her to the airport spilled out over the man's shoes.

To Claudia, it all seemed to happen in ghastly slow motion. Lipsticks, mascara, perfume, hairbrush, mirror, sponge toe dividers for painting toe-nails, the whole panoply of cosmetics, in fact, as well as mints, Biros, her purse, a camera, a travel plug, her Filofax, sunglasses, spare films, a novel, tissues, emery boards, a tiny, knitted teddy bear she had carried around with her since she was a child, keys, old credit card receipts, an earring she had been looking for for ages, dog-eared photographs, a cheap brooch Michael had once given her as a joke, even a change of underwear for the flight...all scattered with gay abandon around the man's feet and under his seat.

Claudia closed her eyes. Please, she prayed, when I open them again, let it not have happened! But when she steeled herself to unscrew her eyes the man was still sitting there, still surrounded by her debris while the empty bag dangled uselessly from her nerveless hand.

With a sigh, he laid his papers on the seat beside him and bent to retrieve her bra from where it had caught on his shoe. Holding it between his fingers, he proffered it to Claudia. 'No doubt you'll need this,' he said.

Mortified, she snatched it from his hand. 'Sorry,' she muttered. Falling to her knees, she began scrabbling beneath his seat, desperately trying to scoop everything back into the bag, but humiliation was making her clumsy, and half of them spilled out again. To make matters worse, instead of moving away to another seat, the man bent to help her, handing her cosmetics and sentimental mementoes with a lack of comment that was somehow more crushing than any sarcasm.

'Flight GF920 to Dubai and Menesset is now ready to board.' To Claudia's intense relief the tannoy crackled into life at last and there was a general stirring of anticipation as the first-class passengers and families with children were invited to board.

'Please, there's no need to bother,' she said through gritted teeth as the man glanced up at the announcement. What was the betting that he was travelling first class? 'You go on. I've got everything now, anyway.'

He straightened, put his papers into his briefcase with an insulting lack of haste compared to her own scramble to refill her bag, and pulled his boarding card from his jacket pocket. He *was* travelling first class, Claudia noted bitterly. Nodding a curt farewell, he turned towards the departure gate, only to stop and stoop to pick up yet another lipstick that had rolled along the floor.

''Nights of Passion'.' He read the end as he handed it back to Claudia. 'You won't want to lose that one, will you? You never know when you might need it.'

And with that final, quite unnecessary shot of sarcasm he walked off, leaving Claudia staring resentfully after him and thinking, much too late of course, of any number of crushing retorts that would have put him in his place.

At least he was flying first class, she reassured herself, so there was no danger that she would find herself sitting next to him, and in all likelihood he would be getting off in Dubai anyway. Claudia didn't like feeling ridiculous, and she was glad to think that she would never again have to set eyes on the one witness to her uncharacteristic lack of poise.

In fact, she could pretend that it had never happened...until she got onto this crummy little plane and realised that she was going to have to spend two and a half hours sitting next to him! Typical of her luck this year, Claudia thought glumly. Being twenty-nine had

been no fun at all and it looked as if her very last day
in her twenties was going to run true to form. Perhaps
she would wake up tomorrow on her thirtieth birthday
and find that things had changed?

Blowing out a tiny sigh, she cast the man a resentful
glance from under her lashes. There had obviously been
no good fairy at *her* christening! If there had been, she
might have organised an attractive, charming man who
would while away the last hours Claudia could get away
with calling herself young. Instead, she was landed with
someone dour and middle-aged. He must be at least
forty, she decided dismissively, so used to thinking of
the forties as a vague time in the future when she would
be galloping through middle age on her way to a bus
pass and a Zimmer frame that it came as something of
a shock to realise that as from the next day, he would
only be ten years older than her.

He didn't *look* as if he was on the verge of cashing
in his pension, it had to be said. Claudia studied him a
little closer. There was a solidity about him, a balanced,
assured air, as if he had grown into his looks and was
completely at ease with himself. It was just a pity his
expression was so formidable. He would be really quite
attractive if he smiled.

She eyed him half speculatively, wondering how he
would respond to a little light flirtation, but when her
gaze stopped at that implacable mouth she decided not
to waste her time trying. There was something decidedly
unflirtable about the way he sat there reading that boring
report with its endless graphs and lists of figures.

But then, she had always liked a challenge, hadn't
she?

Claudia reached for the safety card tucked into the
seat back in front of her and pretended to study it while
she planned her strategy. She didn't hold out too many
hopes of getting a smile out of him, but it would be fun

to prise as much information out of him as possible. If he thought he was going to be able to ignore her for two and a half hours, he had another think coming!

'This plane looks awfully old,' she said, casting around for a way to restart the conversation after his ungentlemanly reference to the incident at Heathrow. 'Do you think it's safe?'

'Of course it's safe,' said David without looking up from his report. He might have known she wouldn't shut up for long! 'Why on earth shouldn't it be?'

'Well, it's so old, for a start,' said Claudia, plucking at the tatty material covering the seats. 'Look at it! This kind of décor went out in the Sixties! Where's this plane been since then?'

'Flying perfectly safely between Menesset and Telama'an, I should think.' Very deliberately, David made a note in the margin to remind her that he wasn't distracted that easily. 'What's wrong with the plane? Apart from the worrying fact that you don't like its colour scheme, of course?'

Claudia looked around her as the plane began to roll backwards from the chocks. There were only about forty other passengers, their seats arranged in pairs on either side of the narrow aisle. 'I didn't realise it would be so small,' she confessed.

David turned a page like a calculated insult. 'Telama'an isn't a big place,' he said with a kind of bored indifference.

'I hope it's big enough to have an airport,' Claudia snapped, irritated by his lack of reaction. 'Or are they going to kit us out with parachutes and push us out when we're over the right spot?'

He did glance at her at that, but it was such a withering look that she wished she had never tried to divert him from his report in the first place. 'Don't be ridiculous,' he said. 'There's been an airstrip there for years,

but this is about the biggest plane that can land there at
the moment. It'll be different when the new airbase is
completed, of course. Telama'an is one of the more remote regions of Shofrar, but it's strategically important
and the government are keen to develop the area. At the
moment, there's nothing but a dusty little oasis in the
middle of the desert, so the local sheikh wants a complete infrastructure: an airbase, roads, a water supply,
power...it's a huge project.'

Oh, dear, one of those men that lectured instead of
answered! Claudia sighed. 'You seem to know a lot
about it,' she said, fanning herself with the safety card
and trying not to think too much about the take-off as
the plane taxied slowly down the runway.

'I should do. We're the contracting engineers on the
project.'

She half turned in her seat to look at him in surprise
and dawning consternation. 'But GKS Engineering are
the contractors, aren't they?'

For his part, David eyed her with deepening misgiv-
ing. What did this silly woman have to do with GKS?
'How do you know that?' he asked suspiciously.

'My cousin's married to the senior engineer on the
project...Patrick Ward. Do you know him?'

David's heart sank. Of course she *would* have to be
going to visit the very people he would normally spend
most time with in Telama'an! Was there to be no getting
away from her? 'Yes, I know Patrick,' he said reluctantly. 'And Lucy.'

'Oh, well, I'll tell them I met you,' said Claudia, who
had not missed the reluctance in his voice and who had
perceived an opportunity to achieve at least one of her
objectives. 'What's your name?' Let him get out of that
one!

'David Stirling,' he admitted after a tiny pause.

'I'm Claudia Cook,' she introduced herself, although

he hadn't asked. Peeping a glance at him from under her lashes, she wondered whether she should force him to shake hands, but decided against it. It had been achievement enough to get a name out of him, and, looking at that jaw, she didn't think that David Stirling was a man she would want to push *too* far. Better to stick to the inane conversation line; it was a far more effective way of needling him!

'So you're an engineer as well, are you?'

'Of sorts.' David was cursing his luck. Not only was he doomed to spend the next two and a half hours sitting next to her, but he couldn't put her in her place as he was longing to do. He was very fond of Lucy and Patrick, so he could hardly tell their guest to shut up and mind her own business. It was hard to believe that there was any connection between them, though. The Wards were one of the nicest couples he knew, while this girl was a ghastly intrusion from some other life altogether.

In spite of himself, he found himself glancing at her. She had beautiful skin—either that, or she was very cleverly made-up. Probably the latter, David decided. Those lashes were too long and thick and dark to be natural with that pale gold hair, and he could see how she had outlined her eyes with a fine pencil.

He had a sudden, bitter picture of Alix at the mirror in his bathroom, her mouth pursed in concentration and one finger holding her eyelid steady as she carefully drew a line above her lashes. David was unprepared for the way the memory could still hurt. Alix had taught him a valuable lesson, and he was wary still of girls like her.

Girls like Claudia Cook.

She would be in marketing, he guessed, or perhaps something in the media. Some job that enabled her to kiss people extravagantly and run around with a clipboard feeling important. She would go to parties and claim to be exhausted by work, although she probably spent most of her day on the phone without producing anything more tangible than a date for lunch or an agreement to talk later.

David smiled grimly to himself. Oh, yes, he had met girls like Claudia before, and he was in no danger at all of being impressed!

The plane had turned, poised for a moment at the end of the runway before hurtling itself down the tarmac and heaving itself into the air at the last moment. Claudia sucked in her breath and concentrated on breathing evenly. David Stirling would only sneer if he thought she was nervous, and she was not going to give him the satisfaction of making a fuss!

Still, it was a relief to hear the tell-tale 'ping' of the 'no smoking' sign being switched off, and as the plane levelled out she turned back to David, only to catch his eyes straying back to his report. She couldn't have him concentrating on his work, could she, now?

'Are you based out in Telama'an like Patrick?' she asked, all eager interest.

'No,' said David through his teeth. The graph danced up and down on the page beneath his eyes. Those wide eyes and that gushing voice didn't fool him for a minute. He knew perfectly well that she had set out to be deliberately provocative for some reason. Well, he wouldn't give her the satisfaction of rising to the bait again. She would soon get bored with cold courtesy. 'I spend most of my time in the London head office.'

'Why are you going to Telama'an now?' Claudia persevered.

He drew a deep breath and forced himself to stay calm. 'I've got a series of extremely important meetings to attend,' he said tightly after a moment. 'We're coming to the end of the first phase of the project, and we want to persuade the government to award us the contract for the next major stage, but there are several other big firms in the running, so we're up against some tough competition.

'The final decision rests with the local sheikh, who is a cousin of the Sultan and who's been given overall responsibility for the project, but he's not an easy man to deal with. After months of requesting a meeting, he's finally offered us the chance to give him a special presentation the day after tomorrow, and it's absolutely vital that I get there as soon as possible to brief the rest of the team before the meeting. However, it does mean that I must check these reports, so if you'll—'

'Well, that's a coincidence!' Claudia interrupted before he could complete his excuse. 'It's absolutely vital that *I* get there by tomorrow as well.'

'Really?' he bit out. 'And why is that?'

She leant towards him confidentially. 'It's my thirtieth birthday tomorrow, and I'm going to a party to meet my destiny!'

David looked at her with incredulity. 'Your *what*?'

'My destiny.' Claudia hoped she looked suitably soulful. 'Years ago a fortune-teller told me that I wouldn't get married until I was thirty, and that I'd meet my husband somewhere where there was a lot of space and sand.'

'So you thought you'd just get on a plane to the desert on the off-chance that you'd bump into some poor unfortunate man?' David didn't even bother to hide his disbelief and she smothered a smile as she opened her eyes wide.

'Oh, *no*. I know exactly who he'll be. The fortune-teller told me that the initials J and D would be very important, so I'm sure I'll be able to recognise him at once. Lucy's going to throw a party so that I meet him on my birthday and all *I* have to do is get there by tomorrow!'

He snorted. 'You're not trying to tell me that Lucy believes any mumbo-jumbo about predictions? I've always thought of her as an intelligent woman!'

'She was there when my fortune was told,' Claudia told him solemnly. 'We were only fourteen and it made a big impression on her,' she added, omitting to mention that both girls had burst giggling out of the tent and Lucy had teased her unmercifully for years afterwards about having to wait until she was thirty before she got married.

At fourteen, thirty had seemed impossibly remote. She had never dreamt that she would actually ever get to be that old, or that she wouldn't be married long before. When she had met Michael, she had even joked with Lucy about thwarting fate and tying the knot at twenty-nine.

Except that Michael hadn't wanted to commit himself in the end—at least not to her—and now here she was, a day short of thirty and just as unwed as the fortune-teller had said she would be.

'You *can't* spend your thirtieth birthday on your own!' Lucy had said when Claudia had rung to tell her that the engagement was finally off.

'I'm so miserable, it doesn't matter what I do,' Claudia had said. 'I can't be bothered to have a party where everyone will just feel sorry for me.'

'Come out to Shofrar, then,' Lucy offered impulsively. 'No one will know anything about Michael, so you could be whoever you wanted to be. It'll be great,' she went on, getting carried away with enthusiasm for the idea. 'We'll have a party on your birthday and you can meet Justin Darke.'

'Justin who?'

'Justin Darke. He's an American architect who's working with Patrick out here, and he is *seriously* attractive. We are talking gorgeous, Claudia! As soon as

I met him I thought he'd be perfect for you—much better than that creep Michael. He's almost disgustingly nice, warm, sincere, *single*...what more could you want?'

'There must be something wrong with him,' said Claudia, whose experience of men had left her armoured against high expectations. Nice, warm, sincere men weren't usually wandering around unmarried without a good reason.

'But there isn't! He's just a great guy,' Lucy insisted. 'And I know he'd like *you*. I showed him your picture the other day and he said you looked like an exciting lady!'

'I don't feel very exciting at the moment,' Claudia said gloomily.

'You just need someone to boost your ego—and Justin's so charming that you wouldn't be able to resist feeling better!'

Claudia was beginning to warm to the idea. 'I suppose it *would* be nice to get away somewhere completely different.'

'Of course it would. A change of scenery, an attractive man...you won't give Michael another thought.' Lucy laughed. 'Hey, remember the fortune-teller at that fête, Claudia? All that business about sand and initials and being thirty? There's certainly plenty of sand out here, and Justin's initials *are* J D...'

'And I'm going to be thirty? Don't remind me!'

'Just think, this could be your big chance to meet your destiny!' said Lucy dramatically, and they both giggled.

'I won't hold my breath,' said Claudia. 'After this last year with Michael I think I can do without destiny—I'll settle for a good time instead!'

It hadn't been easy to take two weeks off at one of the busiest times of the year, but once Claudia had made up her mind to do something she was doggedly determined to succeed, and she had booked her ticket the very next day. Everything seemed to have gone wrong since then, but Claudia had gritted her teeth and told herself it would be worth it when she got off the plane to Lucy's welcoming hug. She was going to have a good time in Telama'an if it killed her...and in the meantime she might as well amuse herself by irritating David Stirling some more!

'You've come all this way in pursuit of a *man* that you've never met but that you just hope will have the right initials?' He was still shaking his head in amazement.

'Why not?' she asked, but he was so appalled at the idea that he missed the teasing glint in her eyes.

'Well, I presumed, since you were travelling alone, that you had some intelligence, even if it is very artfully disguised,' he said caustically. 'Not even someone as desperate as you sound would go all the way to a place like Telama'an without a good reason!'

Claudia considered that after the year she had had the prospect of some sun and some fun and some flattery was reason enough to go anywhere, but that was none of David Stirling's business. 'You don't understand,' she said dramatically. 'I'm at a crossroads in my life! I'm going to be thirty tomorrow, I can't just carry on like before. I've got to seize my opportunities!'

'What opportunities?'

She clutched her throat and somehow managed to keep a straight face. 'To meet my soul mate, of course! JD is waiting for me in the desert...I just know it! All I have to do is fly to him!'

David curled his lip. 'JD? No doubt Lucy has been scouring the compound for someone with the right initials! Has she come up with anyone yet?'

'Maybe,' said Claudia coyly.

'Which poor unfortunate soul has she lined up?' David ran through the possibilities in his mind. 'Jack

Davis? He's married. Jim Denby? Unlikely. Ah!' he said suddenly. '*Justin Darke*! Why didn't I think of him straight away?'

'My lips are sealed,' said Claudia, suddenly realising that in her determination to irritate David Stirling she was running a grave risk of embarrassing Lucy's American friend.

David had seen the flicker in her eyes, though, and drew his own conclusions. Justin Darke was nice enough, but he was no match for a woman like Claudia Cook, that was for sure. Did he have any idea what Claudia and Lucy had planned for him? The first thing he would do when he got to Telama'an was drop a warning word in Justin's ear, although there was something so single-minded about Claudia's attitude that it would take more than a friendly warning to stop her, he was sure.

He shook his head. 'Poor Justin!' he said.

'I really don't know who you're talking about,' Claudia lied. 'And in any case, knowing who I was going to meet would spoil it. All I know is that I'm going to be at that party tomorrow night, and after that I'm leaving it to destiny!'

CHAPTER TWO

DAVID her a sardonic look. 'It looks like you're going to have a busy day being thirty and meeting your destiny tomorrow,' he said, and the unconcealed sarcasm in his voice was enough to provoke a dangerous glitter in Claudia's blue-grey eyes.

'But don't you see? The two are *linked*!' she gushed, hoping that she sounded as ridiculous as she felt. 'Thirty is such a crossroads in one's life, isn't it?'

'Is it?' said David unencouragingly.

'Yes! It's a time to reassess what one wants out of life, a time to change direction, a time to let go of one's youth and face up to the prospect of mortality!'

He turned to her consideringly. 'Do you know,' he said, 'I find it hard to believe that you're going to be thirty tomorrow?'

Claudia was rather taken aback. She didn't think she was looking too bad for her age either, but she hadn't expected a compliment from him. Perhaps she should have tried flirting with him after all? 'Why, thank you—'

'Because,' David interrupted her ruthlessly, 'I never thought that anyone over the age of five could talk such a load of tosh!'

So much for compliments! Bridling, Claudia glared back at him. 'Oh, and I suppose *you* didn't have a crisis at thirty—or can't you remember back that far?' she added nastily.

'I was far too busy to have any crisis.'

She sniffed. 'Well, just wait until you're fifty, that's all! You'll have spent your life working without ever really thinking about what you're doing and why you're doing it, and one day you'll wake up and realise that you're fifty and it's too late to do anything about it. You'll be in crisis then!'

'Possibly,' said David, nettled by her assumption that he was practically past it already, 'but I don't propose to worry about it now. As it happens, I haven't even made it to forty yet! I've still got over a month before I have to deal with *that* crisis!'

'Oh?' Claudia's voice had just the right tone of surprise to be insulting. 'When's your birthday?'

He sighed. 'September the seventeenth.' He knew what was coming next!

'You're a Virgo, then.' Claudia nodded sagely, although she wasn't in fact at all sure when Virgos became Capricorns, or was it Librans? 'That figures.'

David wasn't going to give her the satisfaction of asking *what* figured. All he knew was that she was by far the silliest and most exasperating woman he had ever met, and he wasn't going to indulge her any longer, Lucy's cousin or not.

'I'm sure,' he said dismissively. 'Now, if you'll excuse me, I really do have to do some work.'

'Oh, of *course*!' said Claudia with exaggerated contrition. 'I'm *so* sorry for disturbing you. I'll just read my magazine quietly, and you won't even know I'm here.'

David didn't think *that* was very likely. She was the kind of girl who could sit in a dark room without moving or speaking and still be distracting. Still, if she would just shut up for a while, he might be able to finish that report.

He bent over it and began jotting quick, decisive notes in the margin while Claudia, reduced to pulling out a magazine, tried not to watch him. It was hard not to be impressed by his ability to concentrate as he worked methodically through the report, and in spite of herself her eyes kept sliding sideways to skitter along the force-ful line of his jaw.

He *wasn't* good-looking, not really. He had a hard mouth and lean, intelligent face, but there was an air of restraint about him, as if he deliberately presented him-self in a low key. It was difficult to accuse him of being colourless, though, much as she would have liked to. The strength of his personality was obvious in his calm assurance, in the disconcerting sharpness of his eyes and the intangible quality of authority that clung to him.

He had taken off his jacket, and rolled up the sleeves of his white shirt in a businesslike fashion. Claudia was very conscious of the dark hair on his forearms, and she had to keep hers rigidly together on her lap in case her arm brushed against him. She tried not to look too ob-viously, but out of the corner of her eye she could see the pulse beating in his neck above his open collar, very slow and very steady.

Stealthily, she felt the pulse in her own throat, which was hammering away at a rate of knots. Perhaps she was just highly strung?

Nobody could accuse David Stirling of being highly strung. Did he ever get excited? Claudia's eyes strayed back to his mouth. What would it take to arouse a man like that, to break through the cool control and make that pulse beat faster for once?

Aghast at the train of her own thoughts, she jerked her gaze away and hastily turned a page of the magazine. Oh, God, an article about sex! She couldn't read *that* with him sitting right beside her. Flicking on, she came to a piece about the pleasures and pressures of different ages. No point in reading about the twenties, she thought glumly. She was leaving those behind her. She'd better read about the thirties instead and find out whether there was any life after thirty, or whether she should just give in and get herself some tweeds and a blue rinse.

Women in their thirties have left all the insecurities of the twenties behind. They are poised, confident, at ease with themselves.

Oh, yeah? thought Claudia cynically.

They have learnt what suits them and what doesn't, and have the maturity and sophistication to lead life on their own terms. 'I love women in their thirties,' one man was quoted as saying. 'They're much more interesting than young girls because they've got something to say for themselves, they know what they want and they're confident enough to go out and get it. I think it's by far the sexiest age. So many women grow into their looks in their thirties. They've come to terms with their own bodies and that's what gives them a glamour and assurance that no twenty-year-old could hope to achieve.'

Claudia gave a disbelieving sniff. As David Stirling would say, what a load of tosh! She had never met a woman who had come to terms with her own body, thirty or not! Still, all that sophistication and glamour didn't sound too bad, even if there was something daunting about the idea of maturity. When was it going to hit her?

It was all very well to talk about knowing what you wanted, but all Claudia could think that she really wanted right now was to get to Telama'an, to wash her hair and to have a very long, very cold gin and tonic. Hardly very lofty objectives with which to begin the next decade of her life!

Claudia closed the magazine with a sigh. David was still reading his report. There was something wrong with a man who could concentrate like that, she decided, but she didn't quite dare interrupt him again. That must be

because she was still twenty-nine and not yet confident.
It would be different tomorrow.

Casting around for another diversion, she looked
around the cabin and met the eyes of a Shofrani sitting
across the aisle from her. He was a handsome man,
dressed stylishly in western clothes, with dark hair and
very warm, very dark eyes. He smiled charmingly as
their eyes met and Claudia, pleased to find someone who
seemed disposed to like her after David's crushing attitude, smiled back.

'I am sorry if I was staring,' he said in excellent
English. 'We do not often see such beautiful passengers
on the flight to Telama'an!'

Claudia warmed to his flattery. He introduced himself
as Amil and they were soon embarked on a discreet flirtation. He had been doing business for his uncle in the
capital, he told her, and was now on his way home.

'Will you be staying long in Telama'an?'

'Just a couple of weeks, then I have to go back to
work.'

'Your job cannot spare you for any longer?'

'I'm afraid not. I work for a television production
company and we're terribly busy at the moment.'

Beside her, David, who was unable to avoid listening
in on their irritatingly complacent conversation, awarded
himself points for being right about her job anyway. He
had guessed that she worked in the media, but he might
have known that it would be in television! He tried to
close his ears and focus on his report, but Claudia was
rabbiting on about how hectic and important her job was,
and her new-found friend was just encouraging her, nodding and smiling and sounding impressed. It was hard
to tell which of them was more pleased with themselves,
David thought savagely, and gritted his teeth.

Out of the corner of her eye, Claudia caught the tightening of his jaw, and redoubled her efforts to charm

Amil. She would show him that *some* men found her attractive! Turning back to Amil, she gave him a dazzling smile. 'But that's enough about my job,' she said winsomely. 'I'm sure your life is much more interesting than mine!'

God, she was irritating! David clamped his lips together and scoured out a typing error in the report with unnecessary vigour. He had to endure another quarter of an hour of their stomach-churning, treacly conversation before the steward, moving down the aisle with a trolley, broke them up.

David breathed a sigh of relief, but it was short-lived. Claudia must have had the attention span of a gnat. Couldn't she just sit still for a minute? She was rummaging around in her bag, sorting through her inexhaustible supply of lipsticks, polishing her mirror, carefully applying colour to her mouth.

When she snapped the mirror shut and dropped it back in the bag with her lipstick, David allowed himself to hope that she would relax, but no! Now she had got out an emery board and was touching up a nail, the next minute it was hand cream, the next refreshing herself with a spray of perfume. The subtle, expensive, undeniably sexy scent that he already associated with her drifted towards him, but he resolutely ignored it and, putting down his pen, pretended to consult the index.

Then—of course!—she had to comb her hair. Tipping her head forward, Claudia ran a comb through the silky mass and then tossed her hair back so that it bounced softly around her face. David tried not to notice how soft it looked, or how the sun through the window glinted on the gleaming strands and turned them into spun gold.

At last it seemed as if she was finished. The comb was put away, the bag pushed under the seat once more. David offered up a silent prayer of thanks and picked up his pen again.

Claudia was bored. David was still resolutely ignoring her and she had run out of ways to provoke him. It was no fun if he wouldn't respond, anyway. She glanced at her watch. Still an hour and a half to go. Amil was talking to his neighbour, and the magazine just seemed full of articles expressly designed to remind her how old she was getting. With an impatient sigh, she began drumming her fingers on the arm of the seat.

For David, it was the final straw. He threw down his pen. 'Can't you sit still for two seconds?' he demanded between clenched teeth.

'I am sitting still,' objected Claudia, offended.

'You're not,' said David, hanging onto the shreds of his temper with difficulty. 'If you're not chatting up complete strangers, you're tarting yourself up, combing your hair, admiring yourself in your mirror, or fossicking around in that bag, and then, when you've exhausted all those intellectual activities, you sit there and make that *extremely irritating* noise with your fingers!'

Claudia looked huffy. 'What do you want me to do?'

'I don't want you to do anything! Why can't you just sit quietly?'

'I hate just sitting,' she said sulkily. 'I've got a very low boredom threshold. I've got to do *something*.'

'Why don't you try thinking?' David suggested with an unpleasant look. 'That ought to be a novel experience for you. The effort of using your brain ought to keep you occupied for a good five minutes!'

'I've *been* thinking,' said Claudia, very much on her dignity.

'You amaze me!' He shook his head in mock admiration. 'And what have you been thinking *about*?'

'Well, mostly I've been wondering how Patrick came to give a job to anyone quite so arrogant and unpleasant,' she pretended to confide.

David looked at her for a moment. 'What makes you think Patrick gave me a job?'

'I know he's the senior engineer on the project, so if you're involved with the negotiations you must report to him, and if he knew how badly you represent GKS I don't think he'd be very pleased. Patrick may seem very easygoing,' she swept on, 'but I've known him a long time, and I can tell you that if he felt that you were giving the wrong impression of GKS he would want to do something about it.'

'You don't think he'll sack me before the meetings, do you?'

There was a look in David's eye that Claudia didn't quite like, and she tossed her head. 'I would have thought that depended on you,' she said tartly.

'So if I'm nice to you for the rest of the journey he might let me stay?'

'I wouldn't want to put you to so much effort,' she snapped. 'Being nice obviously doesn't come naturally!'

'That rather depends on who I have to be nice *to*,' said David, but before Claudia could frame a suitably crushing retort her attention was caught by a spluttering noise from the silver wing stretching out from below the window.

'You know, I'm sure there's something wrong with that engine,' she said worriedly. 'It keeps making funny noises.'

'Don't be ridiculous,' said David. 'What could possibly be wrong with it?'

'*I* don't know!' she snapped. 'I don't know anything about engines.'

'Then what makes you think you know whether it's making a funny noise or not?' He made a great show of leaning forward and cupping a hand to his ear. 'It sounds fine to me.'

'That's what they always say,' said Claudia darkly.

'It's just like a disaster film. They always start off showing people doing ordinary things, just like us.'

'There's nothing ordinary about the way you've been behaving since you got on the plane,' David put in, but she ignored him.

'They're all having cups of coffee and chatting, and none of them realise that something terrible is about to happen—but they're all right because they've got Bruce Willis or Tom Cruise or some other hunk to spring into action and save them, and all I've got is a paper-pushing engineer whose only advice is to sit still and keep quiet!'

David had been listening to her with mounting exasperation. 'I have never met anybody who could whip themselves up into a frenzy about absolutely nothing before!'

'It's not nothing! I'm telling you, there's something wrong, I can feel it!'

'For the last time,' said David between his teeth, 'there is nothing the matter with the engine!'

With that the engine spluttered and cut out, and the plane veered sharply to one side. Immediately there was a babble of panic-stricken voices in Arabic as the other passengers were caught unawares by the sudden deceleration.

Instinctively, Claudia clutched at David's hand. He winced as her fingers dug into his flesh, her eyes wide and dark with terror as he enfolded her hand in a warm, strong clasp to forestall any hysterics. 'There's no need to panic,' he said firmly. 'The pilot's bringing the plane round now. Everything's under control.'

The plane had straightened, and the pilot opened the throttle to increase the power to the remaining engine so that it picked up speed once more. There was a burst of Arabic over the intercom and to Claudia, not understanding a word, it sounded terrifying. David was listening closely, and she noted with detached surprise that he spoke Arabic.

'What's he saying?' she whispered.

'He says there's nothing to worry about. We've lost an engine, but there's no problem about flying with one engine, so he's going to head for the nearest airstrip as a precaution and try and sort out the problem there.' David's voice was calm, infinitely reassuring. 'Now you can relax and say "I told you so".'

Claudia moistened her lips. 'I don't think I'll relax until I've got two feet firmly on the ground,' she said unsteadily. 'I'll say it then.'

Afterwards David told her that it had only taken twenty minutes for the pilot to make a long, straight approach and land at a dusty airstrip in the middle of the desert, but for Claudia it seemed that they sat there for an eternity. David kept talking in the same quiet, steady voice, and she clutched at the immeasurable re-assurance of his cool presence without hearing a word that he was saying. All she could think about was how much time she had wasted agonising about turning thirty when she might never make it after all.

When the undercarriage went down with a clunk, she jerked and braced herself for an emergency landing, but in the end the plane touched down so lightly that it was only when the screaming engines quieted and they turned to taxi slowly back down the runway that Claudia let herself believe that they had landed safely. Closing her eyes and letting out a long breath, she slumped back in her seat.

When she opened them again, the plane had stopped. Outside, the heat wavered over the tarmac and bounced off the silver wings. There were a couple of prefabricated buildings, a ramshackle control tower and a few dusty buildings straggling along the road that led off into the heat haze.

Claudia licked her lips and tried her voice very cautiously. 'Where are we?'

'A place called Al Mishrah,' said David, looking out of the window with a jaundiced eye. 'There used to be a big gas terminal here, hence the airport, but it's disused now and they only get the occasional flight serving what's left of the town.'

'Not your ideal stopover, then,' said Claudia with an effort.

The corner of David's mouth lifted as if in acknowledgement of her feeble attempt at a joke. 'You could say that.'

'Wh-what happens now?'

He sighed. 'On past experience of Shofrar, I'd say nothing much.'

He was right. Some of the other passengers were standing up, shouting and gesticulating, but it was several minutes before a set of steps were produced and wheeled across the tarmac towards the waiting plane. It was suffocatingly hot, and Claudia longed for some fresh air, but as soon as the door swung open the smell of fuel rolled on a wave of heat through the cabin, and she wrinkled her nose in distaste.

Immediately there was a scrum of passengers pushing to get out, but there seemed little point in hurrying, and it was not until the first crush had subsided that David turned to Claudia. 'Do you feel OK now?'

'Yes, I'm fine.'

'In that case, do you think I could have my hand back?'

'Oh!' Claudia dropped his hand as if it had stung her and her cheeks flamed with mortification. 'I'm sorry,' she muttered, flustered. 'I didn't realise; that is...I forgot...'

'It's all right.' David's cool voice broke across her

embarrassed stutterings as he tucked his report back into his briefcase and stood up.

Claudia hesitated, cringing at the thought that she had sat for so long clinging to his hand like a little girl. He must think she was absolutely pathetic, but she could hardly ignore his patience. 'You've been very kind,' she said a little stiffly. 'Thank you.'

David was conscious of a feeling of surprise as he followed her down the aisle. He had expected her to take any attention as her due and he was disconcerted to find how pleased he was that he had misjudged her.

Inside the prefabricated hut that obviously served as a terminal it was hardly much cooler than outside. A single ceiling fan slapped at the air without enthusiasm and the room resonated with the aggrieved clamour of angry passengers. David and Claudia sat on orange plastic chairs that were cracked and dusty with neglect and waited.

At first Claudia was too relieved to find herself alive and back on solid ground again to fret much at the lack of action and she was content just to sit next to David, intimidated more than she wanted to admit by the heat and the glare and this dingy building where nothing seemed to work and she had no idea what was going on.

Claudia didn't like feeling out of control, and she was uncomfortably aware that, arrogant and unpleasant as David might be, his cool, contained presence was immeasurably reassuring.

The long minutes ticked slowly by. Claudia sat and looked at a poster advertising what she guessed to be some kind of soft drink that had faded in the harsh light to a pale, washed-out blue. Flies zoomed through the oppressive heat and buzzed frantically near her ears until she waved them away in disgust, and she could feel the plastic, sticky and uncomfortable through her thin trousers.

As her impatience grew, she shifted irritably in the chair and glanced at her watch for the umpteenth time. They had been sitting there for nearly an hour. 'What's happening?' she burst out at last.

David, who had just been thinking that a severe fright considerably improved her, sighed. He might have known that she wouldn't be able to sit still and silent much longer. 'The pilot and a couple of local ground crew are looking at the engine. We're waiting for him to come back and tell us what's going to happen—' He broke off as a stir of expectation marked the entrance of the harassed-looking pilot. 'Ah, here he is now.'

Claudia jumped to her feet. 'Let's go and see what's going on!'

'*I'll* go and talk to him,' said David firmly. 'You wait here.'

She opened her mouth to object, but something in his face made her close it again, and subside back onto her seat.

She watched David as he walked over to the pilot. He was tall and lean, and he moved easily, with a sort of balanced, economical grace that made her think queerly of a cat, or an athlete focusing on the race ahead. The other men seemed to recognise the authority of his presence, for they parted instinctively to let him through.

Claudia could only see his back as he stood talking to the pilot, but judging by the other man's frustrated gestures and the reactions of those listening the news was not good, and David's expression was grim when he turned at last and made his way back to her.

'The plane's being taken out of service,' he said as he came up. 'They're going to divert the next flight to pick us up.'

'Oh, well, that's something, I suppose,' said Claudia, who had been expecting much worse. 'When's it arriving?'

'Not for another two days.'

'Two days?' She stared at him in gathering wrath as his words sank in. *Two days?*

David shoved his hands in his pockets and sighed with frustration. 'There's nothing wrong with your hearing, anyway,' he said.

'But...but they can't expect us to spend *two days* in this dump!'

'There's some kind of hotel in the town, apparently, probably left over from the boom days, so it's likely to be a bit run-down.'

'I don't care if they've got the Ritz,' snapped Claudia. 'It's my birthday tomorrow and I'm not staying here! Why can't they send another plane now?'

'Shofrar isn't geared up for tourism. This is just a small internal airline, and all their other planes have got scheduled flights of their own.'

'Great!' Claudia leapt to her feet and began pacing up and down with her arms folded. 'There must be something we can do! What about a bus?'

'I think it's highly unlikely that there would be much of a service between here and Telama'an. We've had to divert way off course to land here.'

'All right, a taxi, then?'

'This isn't Piccadilly, Claudia. You can't just flag down a taxi and ask it to drive you off into the desert. There aren't even any metal roads around here.'

'What, then?' she demanded impatiently. 'How can you just *stand* there and do nothing?'

David looked down his nose. He much preferred her when she was scared. 'I can't see that working myself up into a frenzy, as you seem to do at the slightest provocation, would magically produce a plane,' he said repressively.

'You mean you're not going to do anything?' said

Claudia in disgust. 'What about your meeting? I thought you wanted to get to Telama'an as much as I do!'

'I've got every intention of getting there as soon as possible,' he said with a cool look. 'If you were prepared to shut up and just listen for a change, you would have heard me say that I was going to try and get hold of a vehicle. I doubt very much if there will be anything suitable to hire, but it might be possible to buy something.'

'Buy a car?' She looked at him blankly. 'But—'

'But what?'

'Well…' She hesitated. 'You can't just set out across the desert in a car, can you?'

'You can if you know what you're doing,' said David. 'And fortunately I do. I've spent some time in Shofrar, and I'm quite capable of getting myself to Telama'an.'

Had there been a stress on that 'myself'? Claudia fiddled with her ring and wished she hadn't been quite so forthright in her opinion of him earlier on. 'Um…I haven't got very much money with me,' she said awkwardly. 'But if you would give me a lift I'm sure Patrick would give you half the cost, and then I'd be able to pay him back when I got to London. I'd be very grateful.'

She looked at him pleadingly. 'Please,' she added.

She really did have extraordinary eyes, David found himself thinking. They were somewhere between blue and grey, a deep, soft, smoky colour, like twilight over the hills, the kind of eyes a man could lose himself in, the kind of eyes that could make him forget to breathe.

He dragged his gaze away. Claudia was everything he disliked in a girl. She was silly and superficial. She had irritated and exasperated and deliberately provoked him, and he knew perfectly well that he would be ready to murder her long before they reached Telama'an. Just because she had beautiful eyes that played odd tricks with his breathing, it was no reason to take her with him. If he had any sense, he would just say no.

'Oh, all right,' he said irritably. 'But no complaining! It'll be a hard trip and if I have to listen to any moaning you can get out and walk!'

'*Thank* you!' Claudia's face lit up with a smile that stopped the breath in David's throat. He hadn't seen her smile before and he was taken aback to discover how it illuminated her face and deepened the blue in her eyes. 'You won't regret it,' she promised. 'I won't say a word,' she offered generously. 'I'll do whatever you say.'

'I'll believe that when I see it!' David thrust his hands deeper into his pockets and scowled at the poster on the wall, infuriated by his own reaction. Damn it, the last thing he needed right now was to start noticing how much younger and warmer and lovelier she looked when she smiled. The meeting in Telama'an was vital to the future of the firm and it was that he should be concentrating on, not pretty eyes or unexpected smiles!

'I'll go and see what I can find out,' he added in a brusque voice. 'Stay there.'

'All right.' Claudia was too relieved at his agreement to object to his tone. For a nasty moment there she had thought he was going to refuse, and she couldn't really have blamed him. They hadn't exactly got off on the right foot. She was determined to be nice to him from now on, though.

She waited obediently until David returned, but as soon as she saw his face she knew that he hadn't had any success. 'I've had a word with a few people,' he said. 'It might be possible to fix something up, but I can't do anything until we get into town. Apparently they're trying to arrange some kind of bus, so in the meantime we're just going to have to wait.'

'I seem to have spent this entire trip waiting,' sighed Claudia, and he glared at her, still resentful of the effect her smile had had on him.

'I thought you weren't going to complain!'

'That wasn't a complaint, it was a comment,' she muttered, but lapsed into a sullen silence rather than get into an argument with him. She had promised to be nice, and she wouldn't put it past him to leave her behind after all!

Sighing, she crossed her legs in an effort to get comfortable, then uncrossed them when it didn't work. A few moments later, she tried crossing them the other way.

'For God's sake, stop fidgeting!' hissed David.

Claudia opened her mouth to tell him she was bored and uncomfortable, but thought better of it. 'I've got cramp in my leg,' she said placatingly. 'I'll just walk around a bit.'

She wandered over to the window and stood for a while watching the luggage being unloaded off the plane onto a decrepit trolley. As she watched, she saw Amil, the man who had been sitting across the aisle from her, walk purposefully over and pick out a bag. He looked like a man who knew where he was going, and Claudia waved at him as he came back through the terminal.

'Aren't you waiting for the bus?'

'I am fortunate in having family contacts here,' he explained. 'I need to be in Telama'an by tomorrow, so one of my relatives has brought me out a car. If I set out now, I think I will be able to make it in time.'

'Oh, you are lucky!' sighed Claudia enviously. 'It looks as if we're going to be here for ages yet.'

'You are anxious to get to Telama'an?'

'I have to be there by tomorrow.'

'Then why do you not come with me?' Amil suggested. 'It will be a long and uncomfortable trip, and it will mean spending the night at an oasis, but if you want to be in Telama'an by tomorrow I would be more than happy to take you.'

'Go with you?' Claudia hesitated, her mind working quickly as she considered his offer. Amil seemed charming, but he was a stranger and she knew nothing about the customs in Shofrar. It would be hopelessly naive to entrust herself to him.

On the other hand, she couldn't bear to waste two days of her precious holiday sitting around in this terrible place if David didn't manage to get hold of a car. She *couldn't* spend her birthday alone here, and Amil's offer might be her only chance to get to Telama'an in time.

She couldn't risk it, though. 'It's terribly kind of you...' she was beginning when she caught sight of David over Amil's shoulder. He was sitting on the orange plastic chairs, looking as tough and self-contained as ever, but his jaw was tight and she had the impression that even his cool was beginning to fray, and Claudia's words trailed off even as she tried to frame a polite excuse.

Of course! The answer was so obvious that she couldn't believe she hadn't thought of it straight away. 'It's *terribly* kind of you,' she said again to Amil with a warm smile. 'We'd love to come with you. I'll just go and tell my husband the good news!'

CHAPTER THREE

THERE was a tiny pause. Amil's own smile, which had broadened as she rushed into eager acceptance, froze just a fraction. 'Your husband?'

'David.' Claudia was all innocent surprise. 'Didn't you realise I was married?'

'No.' Amil pulled himself together. 'You must forgive my surprise,' he apologised. 'It was just that I had the impression that you were travelling alone when we talked before.'

'I'm sorry, I should have introduced you,' said Claudia, looking suitably penitent. 'He was sitting next to me on the plane. I'm a terrible coward about flying and he had to hold my hand all the way down.'

It was obvious that Amil was remembering, and Claudia congratulated herself on a convincing touch. 'That was your husband?' he said.

'Of course,' she said, opening her eyes wide. 'I would hardly hold hands with a perfect stranger, would I?'

'Of course not.' Amil smiled. Claudia could almost see him giving a mental shrug at a lost opportunity and deciding to make the best of it. 'In any case, I shall be delighted to give both you and your husband a lift.'

She had to give him full marks for courtesy. Perhaps there hadn't been any need to lie after all? Still, it was too late now.

'You're very kind,' she said, and meant it. 'When were you planning to leave?'

'As soon as possible.'

'Then I'll go and find David at once.' Claudia smiled again. 'I won't be a minute.'

From the other side of the room, David saw her hurrying towards him, all smiles. He was prepared for the effect this time, though, and had time to rigidly control his breathing as she rushed up.

'Why are you looking so pleased with yourself?'

'*I*,' Claudia announced smugly, 'have got us both a lift to Telama'an, leaving right now!'

'You've done what?' David looked incredulous.

'Amil's going to drive us there.'

'Who the hell is Amil?'

'He was sitting across the aisle from me on the plane,' she said, thinking that he could have seemed a little more pleased at her news.

'Oh, yes,' said David unpleasantly. 'The man you were flirting with so outrageously. Why didn't you say?'

'Well, if I *was* flirting,' said Claudia in a voice of honeyed sweetness, 'I was flirting with the right man, and it's paid off. He's got a car waiting outside right now.'

'How did he manage that?' David was still suspicious, and she clicked her tongue in exasperation.

'He's got contacts here and pulled a few strings. What does it matter, anyway?' she demanded impatiently. 'The important thing is that he needs to be in Telama'an tomorrow as well, and he's got room to take us with him.'

David stared at her almost accusingly. 'Why am I included in this generous invitation? I haven't exchanged so much as a word with the man, and after the way you were batting your eyelashes at him I would have thought that the last thing he wanted was to have me along to play gooseberry!'

'Ah, well, I was just coming to that.' Claudia manoeuvred him round so that his expression was hidden from the rest of the room. She lowered her voice. 'I, er, told Amil you were my husband.'

'You did *what*?' David's voice rose to a shout and she shushed him frantically.

'I told Amil we were married,' she whispered fiercely.

'What in God's name made you do that?' he demanded furiously.

'I had to.' Claudia glanced around, terrified that Amil would come bearing down on them before she had had a chance to brief David. 'I couldn't go off with him on my own, could I? I don't know anything about him other than the fact he's got a vehicle.'

'You don't know anything about me, but it doesn't seem to have stopped you claiming me as a husband!'

'You know Patrick and Lucy,' she pointed out. 'So I sort of know you by proxy. Anyway,' she swept on when David continued to look unconvinced, 'I'd have thought you'd have been grateful!'

'Grateful? Grateful at being forced into pretending to be married to someone like you?' David was furious. How dared she involve him in her stupid masquerade? The sheer arrogance of the woman was phenomenal! Even Alix would have thought twice before appropriating a perfect stranger to act as her husband without so much as a by-your-leave! 'You must be joking!'

'Look,' said Claudia grittily, 'you said you wanted to get to Telama'an by tomorrow and this is the best chance you're going to get. Even if you can get hold of a suitable vehicle, we've still got to wait for the bus to take us into town and that might take ages. And then you've got to find a car and make all the arrangements…it could be midnight before all that gets done. We could be well on our way with Amil by then! And what happens if there *isn't* a car? We'll end up spending two days here when we could be at Telama'an.'

She could see David hesitating and decided to try for a spot of emotional blackmail. 'Please come. I'm going to be thirty tomorrow, and I *can't* spend my birthday here!'

'Or miss the chance to fulfil your destiny with Justin Darke?' he added snidely.

Claudia was beginning to wish that she had never teased him with that stupid story but she didn't have time to put him right now. 'We both want to get to Telama'an as soon as possible, don't we?' she said urgently instead. 'This is the obvious answer.'

'The only thing obvious to me is how some women are prepared to go to any lengths to get their man!' said David, who was torn between wanting to get on the road as soon as possible and outrage at the methods Claudia was employing to get her own way. It would serve her right if he refused point-blank to have anything more to do with her!

Claudia cast another frenzied glance over her shoulder. By the door, Amil caught her eye, waved in acknowledgement, and began making his way through the crowd towards them.

Almost weeping with frustration, she turned back to David. If he wanted her to beg, she would beg. '*Please* come,' she pleaded. 'You must see that I can't go on my own, and it's not as if you would have to do anything.'

'Except look like the kind of fool who would marry you!'

'Oh, please say yes!' Claudia threw pride to the wind and David braced himself for the effect of those great, blue-grey eyes. 'He'll be here any second. Please, please, please, *please*!'

'Ah, there you are! I thought I had lost you!' Amil was too well-mannered to look impatient as he came up to them, and Claudia turned to him with a bright, desperate smile.

'I'm sorry I've been so long. I was just, um, telling my husband about your kind offer.' She risked a glance

at David who was looking wooden. Claudia took a deep
breath and prayed that he wouldn't let her down. 'Amil,
this is my husband, David Stirling.'

There was a frozen pause that seemed to Claudia to
last for ever. She didn't dare look at David again. David
himself was rigid with distaste at the embarrassing situation he had found himself in. Damn it, it wasn't fair of
her to embroil him in her ridiculous lies and then stand
there *looking* like that, blue-grey eyes apprehensive,
slender body taut, but her bearing almost gallant as she
waited to hear whether he would denounce her as a liar
or not.

What would she do if he told Amil that he had never
met her before that morning, and wouldn't marry her if
somebody paid him? He wouldn't put it past her to burst
into tears, and David's masculine soul quailed at the
thought. Wouldn't the ensuing scene be even more embarrassing than pretending that she was indeed his wife?
And she was right about one thing. He *did* want to get
to Telama'an...

'How do you do?' he said, and put out his hand with
a sinking sense of having passed the point of no return.
'It's very generous of you to offer to take us with you.
I hope it's not putting you to too much trouble?'

'Not at all,' said Amil courteously as the two men
shook hands. 'I will be glad of the company.'

Limp with relief, Claudia let out her breath in a long
sigh that made Amil glance at her in concern. 'We have
a long drive ahead of us. I am anxious to get to
Telama'an as soon as possible, so I was planning to
leave straight away, but if you are tired....?' He trailed
off interrogatively and she hastened to reassure him.

'We're not in the least tired,' she said firmly. 'All we
want is to get there too.' She glanced at David. 'Don't
we, darling?' she added, prompted by sheer mischief.

David was poker-faced. 'We can't get there soon

enough as far as I'm concerned,' he agreed, with a meaningful glance at Claudia.

'Good.' If Amil was puzzled by the atmosphere between them, he was too polite to show it. 'Well,' he said, opening his hands, 'the car is outside. I will wait for you there while you get your cases.'

David hardly waited until he was out of earshot before he turned on Claudia. 'What's with all this darling stuff?' he accused.

'Oh, married people always call each other darling,' she said gaily as they headed out to find their luggage, in high good humour now that he had agreed to the deception. 'I thought it would sound convincing.'

He snorted in disgust. 'Convincing or not, if you think I'm going to call you darling for the next twenty-four hours, you've got another think coming!'

Claudia stopped dead in mock dismay. 'Don't you love me any more?' she said, and pretended to wobble her lower lip.

David was not amused. 'I'm not in the mood to play silly games,' he warned. 'If it wasn't for the fact that he's ready to leave right now, I'd have told Amil just what an unscrupulous liar you are and left you to talk your own way out of it!'

'Oh, don't be so grumpy,' she said, unimpressed. 'At least we don't have to sit around here waiting for some non-existent bus to turn up.'

'I'm beginning to think anything would be preferable to putting up with you calling me darling,' said David dourly, but Claudia only grinned.

'Come and get your case—darling!'

Pushing their way out through the press of people, they found Amil waiting in front of the terminal next to a shabby but serviceable pick-up truck. He was talking to a couple of men, but raised his hand in farewell and came over to meet David and Claudia as they appeared.

'I am afraid the cases will have to go in the back,' he apologised. 'There is only room for the three of us in the cab.'

Remembering what Alix had been like when faced with the slightest discomfort, David waited for Claudia to shriek in protest when she saw how dusty her smart case was going to get in the open back of the truck, but to his surprise she cheerfully handed over her bag and clambered into the cab. Nor did she make a fuss about the tatty seat or the ominous wheezing of the engine as Amil started it up. Reluctantly, David gave her credit for good manners when it mattered.

In fact, Claudia was so euphoric at the prospect of getting away from Al Mishrah that she would have been happy travelling in a dustcart. After the year she had had, when everything that could go wrong had gone wrong, spending her thirtieth birthday alone in Al Mishrah would have been the final straw, but now that she was on her way to Lucy and the party waiting for her at Telama'an it was as if life had finally decided to give her a break after all, and this journey was a symbol that things would work out from now on. Perhaps she wouldn't even mind being thirty after all, she thought, and as the terminal with its hated orange chairs receded into the distance her spirits soared.

'How long do you think it will take us to get to Telama'an?' she asked Amil.

'It depends on the roads,' he told her. 'It is too hot for tarmac out here, so the roads are little more than tracks across the desert. Sometimes sand covers the track, or it gets so rutted that you have to try another route and risk getting bogged down in soft sand, but if all goes well we should make it to a tiny oasis called Sifa tonight. It's perhaps four hours to there from here, and then another twelve, maybe thirteen hours tomorrow.'

Again, David braced himself for Claudia's horrified protest, and again she surprised him. 'We'll have to hope we don't have too many punctures,' was all she said. He could see her mentally calculating what time they might arrive in Telama'an. No doubt working out how many hours she would have in hand to seduce Justin Darke, he thought sourly, and without knowing why shifted irritably in his seat.

The cab was really only designed for two people to travel in comfort. Amil as the driver had a seat to himself, but David and Claudia were squeezed onto what was effectively a seat and a half, and it was impossible to avoid touching each other. As it was, David was pressed as far against the door as he could go to give Claudia a little more room, and he had turned slightly to rest his arm along the back of the seat. It meant that his hand lay tantalisingly close to the curtain of blonde hair. When he breathed in, he could smell her elusive fragrance, and every time the truck jolted over a corrugation he could feel the warmth of her body as it was thrown against his.

'The truck has air-conditioning, but that is all that can be said for it,' said Amil ruefully as they lurched over a particularly deep rut. 'Not the most comfortable vehicle for roads like these.'

'Never mind,' said Claudia, still buoyant. 'We'll be so glad to stay still that we won't care where we sleep tonight.'

'I'm glad you say that.' Amil grimaced. 'There is a small guest house at Sifa, but it isn't a place that gets tourists and the rooms are very basic.'

'We don't mind,' she assured him, and peeped a naughty glance at David. 'We don't care where we are as long as we're together!'

'If I had so beautiful a wife, I would not mind where I was either,' said Amil gallantly.

Knowing how much it would irritate David, Claudia simpered and leant winsomely against him. 'Can you believe it, darling?' she said, rewarded with a glimpse of a muscle beating in his rigid cheek. 'Amil didn't even realise we were married until I told him!'

'Extraordinary,' David managed to bite out.

'The truth is,' she went on, turning confidentially back to Amil, 'we were having a row, our first argument really, so that's why we were ignoring each other.'

David glared at her. 'I'm sure Amil isn't interested in our little disagreements, *darling*,' he put in quickly before she could make up any more stupid stories.

'Have you been married long?' Amil asked tactfully after a moment.

'Yes,' said David, just as Claudia said 'No'.

There was a tiny pause.

'He's just saying that because it feels as if we've been together for ever,' Claudia said with a laugh that she was pretty sure would set David's teeth on edge. 'The truth of the matter is that we only got married last week.'

'Last week! Then this is a honeymoon for you?'

David suppressed a shudder and got in before Claudia. 'No,' he said firmly. 'I'm here on business, and Claudia wanted to see a cousin who is living in Telama'an, so it seemed a good idea if she came with me on this occasion.'

'Oh, David, darling, you fibber!' Claudia pretended to pout. 'You know you couldn't bear to leave me behind!'

Amil was concentrating on negotiating a heavily rutted section of track, and David took the opportunity to glower ferociously at Claudia, who took not the slightest bit of notice and only pretended surprise when he kicked her foot.

'Mind my foot!' she said innocently.

'Are you in the television business as well, David?'

asked Amil as the truck bumped out onto level track once more.

'Good God, no!' he said in undisguised horror. 'I'm a civil engineer.'

'Ah, you are involved, then, with the new airbase at Telama'an?'

Amil clearly knew about the project, and for a while the two men talked in technicalities that literally went over Claudia's head. She let them talk, content to sit and feel that every inch was taking her closer to Lucy, and to concentrate on not noticing how lean and hard David's body felt whenever the pick-up lurched and flung her against him. She tried thinking instead about how wonderful it was going to be when she arrived at last on Lucy's doorstep tomorrow evening. It would be worth this whole ghastly journey to see Lucy's face and to feel wanted and welcome again.

Letting her mind drift, she amused herself by wondering what Justin Darke would be like. She hoped he would be as charming as Lucy had made him out to be; she could do with a bit of uncritical admiration for a change. Until today, she had had a very clear image of Justin in her mind, but now when she tried to conjure it up David's features intruded irritatingly.

She had only known him a matter of hours, and already she could picture his face in unnerving detail: the cool line of his cheek, the watchful grey eyes, that stern mouth... It was funny to think that she had thought him rather ordinary-looking when she had first seen him. She wouldn't call him handsome, but he certainly wasn't ordinary!

They drove on and on and on along a straight track that stretched out neverendingly towards the horizon, where the sun was setting in a fiery display of red and orange. Mesmerised by the unchanging scenery, Claudia's head began to loll with the motion of the truck as it dipped and swayed around the deeper ruts or juddered over the corrugations.

David glanced down at her. She was almost asleep. His eyes rested on the sweep of her lashes against her cheek, and he wondered what she had been thinking about for so long. Dreaming about Justin Darke? For some reason the idea made him scowl. There was nothing wrong with Justin, but he wasn't nearly man enough to handle Claudia. She would walk all over him, David decided. Look at the fine mess she had landed *him* in!

It was hard to believe that he had only known her for a matter of hours. Already she seemed intensely— exasperatingly—familiar to him, as if her scent and the soft, shimmering hair, the stubborn tilt of her chin and the dogged determination to get her own way were somehow part of his life. She was so like Alix, with her glamour and her assurance, but Alix hadn't had that gleam of mischief in her eyes. Nor would she ever have consented to travel in a vehicle like this without complaint, David thought. Not that Alix would have been stupid enough to chase halfway across the world to meet an unknown man in the hope of finding a husband! She had been more than capable of finding a husband at home, he remembered bitterly.

He looked at Claudia's nodding head. If she wanted to sleep, why didn't she just lean her head back? he wondered irritably, ignoring the fact that she would have had to rest against his outstretched arm. The truck lurched sideways and she swayed towards him, jerking awake at the last minute and straightening with a shake of her head, only to let her eyelids droop once more.

'Oh, for God's sake!' David muttered to himself, and almost fiercely put his arm around her and pulled her into his shoulder. Claudia tried drowsily to resist, but she was too sleepy to put up much of a struggle, and there was something inexpressibly comforting about the strong arm holding her steady against the endless jolting.

David shifted in his seat to give her more room, and she settled quite naturally against him, turning her face into his throat with a tiny murmur. In the darkness, David was preternaturally aware of her breathing, soft and slow against his skin, and without really being aware of what he was doing he rested his cheek against her hair.

Amil glanced across, saw that Claudia was sleeping and pitched his voice low so as not to wake her. 'You are very lucky to have such a wife,' he said to David. 'This is one of the roughest roads in the country and she is obviously very tired, but she has not complained once.'

David felt Claudia's warm, relaxed weight against him. 'No, she hasn't.'

A faint envious sigh escaped Amil. 'She is very beautiful,' he went on, and without thinking David's arm tightened almost jealously around her. He thought about Claudia, her smoky eyes and her smile and the way the sun shimmered in her hair.

'Yes, I suppose she is,' he said slowly.

Amil was plainly disappointed at such a restrained, English response. It seemed very odd that a man with such a lovely wife should be so much more comfortable talking about business!

'It's not much further to the oasis. I just hope that there will be room at the guest house. Unfortunately there are no tourists in this part of the country and as a result no hotels.'

'No.' David half smiled. 'We're going to be building a hotel in Telama'an during the fourth phase of the project, but that will be too late to be of much use to me.'

'Where *do* you stay?' asked Amil. 'I know that some

houses have been built for the expatriate engineers near the site. Do you stay with your colleagues?'

'Usually, yes, but this time Sheikh Saïd has very kindly invited me to stay in the guest quarters at his palace.'

Amil glanced sideways in surprise. 'You are going to stay with my uncle? I did not realise!'

David lifted his cheek from Claudia's head with a jerk. 'Your uncle?' he said carefully.

'Did I not say? Yes, it seems that we are all going to exactly the same place! If my uncle has invited you to stay, then you are honoured guests,' said Amil seriously.

In the darkness, David grimaced. If Amil was going to the palace as well, then he and Claudia could hardly part company as soon as they reached Telama'an. Amil would doubtless mention the fact that they had travelled together, and then it might be difficult to explain what he had done with his supposed wife.

David's mind worked quickly. 'Of course, Claudia and I got married at such short notice that the sheikh does not realise that I am not travelling on my own. It would be discourteous of me to turn up with an unexpected wife, and as I will be working all day anyway we felt in the circumstances that it would be best if she stayed with her cousin.'

'That will not be necessary,' said Amil warmly. 'I know that my uncle will be delighted to offer hospitality to your new wife as well.'

'I wouldn't dream of imposing—' David began, but the other man lifted a deprecating hand.

'It will be no imposition. Hospitality is an honoured tradition in Shofrar, and my uncle would be offended to think that your wife did not want to stay in the palace.'

David had one last try. 'I certainly would not want to offend, but perhaps Sheikh Saïd will understand that it will be difficult for Claudia to visit her cousin as often as she wants from the palace. As you know, the engineers live some way from the town, and without a car—'

'That problem is easily solved,' Amil insisted. 'My uncle has plenty of cars. I am absolutely certain that he will put one at your disposal so that you and your wife are able to come and go as you please while you are staying at the palace.'

Stymied, David could do nothing but set his teeth and put the best possible face on it. 'You are very kind,' he said, hoping that he didn't sound as dismayed as he felt.

They drove on in silence, David storing up everything he was going to say to Claudia as soon as he got her on her own. She was the one who had told Amil they were married, David thought savagely. Amil would doubtless tell his uncle and before they knew where they were they would end up married for the whole of Claudia's visit! He was looking forward to seeing Claudia's face when she heard about *that*!

Claudia didn't wake until the truck bumped to a halt outside a low, flat-roofed building. She stirred and sighed as Amil got out to see about some rooms, and lay blinking, disorientated by the darkness, while she tried to work out where she was and what she was doing.

'Wake up, Claudia.' David's voice brought back memory in a rush, and she jerked upright as if he had dashed a bucket of cold water in her face.

What was she doing snuggled up against *David Stirling*? 'I'm sorry, I—didn't realise... I didn't mean to fall asleep on you,' she stammered.

'At least I didn't have to put up with you calling me darling,' said David dourly to cover the inexplicable sense of loss he had felt as she'd wrenched herself away from him.

Amil had been conducting a rapid conversation in Arabic with someone through the door of the guest house, and now he turned and came back to the truck.

'They have two rooms, but I am afraid they will be very basic.'

Basic was the word. Claudia and David were shown into a white-washed room equipped with a straight-backed chair, a cracked basin and a single iron bedstead, and lit by the dim light of a naked bulb. Claudia's dismayed gaze travelled over the bare walls and distinctly grubby floor and came to a dead stop at the bed. It had never occurred to her that there wouldn't be two beds. Surely she and David weren't going to have to share *that*?

David could read her expression without difficulty. It was left to him to assure the owner of the guest house that the room was fine, and he closed the door firmly after him. 'I hope you're satisfied now,' he said.

Claudia sank onto the chair and looked at the bed in dismay. 'What are we going to do?'

'I don't know about you, but I'm going to wash and then I'm going to get some sleep,' said David, who was tired and irritable and not in the mood to cope with her having a fit about sharing the bed.

'I meant about the bed,' she said, as he had known she would.

'It was your bright idea to pretend that we were married,' he pointed out disagreeably. 'What did you expect, a room of your own?'

'I didn't expect to end up sharing a bed like that,' said Claudia sullenly. 'I suppose a couple of stick insects might find it comfortable if they didn't mind a squash, but it's not big enough for one human, let alone two!'

David rolled his eyes at her exaggeration and opened his case in search of his washbag. 'What do you want me to do about it?' he demanded unhelpfully.

'Couldn't we ask if there's another bed somewhere?'

'If there is, Amil will have it. Now, if you want to knock on his door and ask him to give up his bed for you because you don't feel like sleeping with the man you've told him is your husband, you go ahead, but don't ask me to go with you. I think he's done enough for us today.'

Claudia jumped to her feet to prowl around the room, hugging her arms nervously together. 'We must be able to do *something*. Perhaps they've got a spare mattress they could put on the floor?'

'This isn't the kind of place that has a spare anything.' David sucked in his breath in exasperation. 'Anyway, you wouldn't last five minutes on the floor with the cockroaches running all over you!'

As if on cue, a cockroach scuttled out from behind the basin and Claudia recoiled in horror. 'Ugh!' She shuddered and glanced at David. 'You don't look like the kind of man who's afraid of a few creepy-crawlies, though,' she tried. 'Perhaps you could sleep on the floor?'

'Why the hell should I?' he said with a scowl. '*I* haven't spent the last two hours sleeping like a baby! I haven't got any feeling left in my arm after acting as your pillow, so if sharing a bed bothers you that much sit on the chair all night. I need some sleep.'

He was stripping off his shirt without embarrassment, tossing it onto his case and testing the taps at the basin. They clanked and rattled, grudgingly producing a dribble of murky-looking water after a while. To David's surprise, there was even a plug. He shoved it in and watched the basin fill with a dour expression.

Claudia was very aware of his naked torso. She wanted to be as unselfconscious as he was, but she simply wasn't used to sharing rooms with men she had only met that day. Especially not men like David Stirling, who had riled her from the first and was now making her feel as gauche and uncomfortable as a schoolgirl on her first date. Oh, to be one of those glamorous, self-assured women in their thirties who would no doubt know just how to deal with the situation! The minutes might be ticking away until she reached the third decade of her life, but as far as composure went Claudia still felt firmly in her twenties, if not her teens.

What was it about him that got under her skin? She folded her arms crossly and tried to look interested in the cracked and peeling plaster, but her eyes kept sliding treacherously back to where David stood, rubbing his neck wearily with his hand and clearly completely unperturbed by *her* presence.

He had a nice body, she admitted to herself grudgingly: powerful shoulders, lean hips, a broad, sleek back. A memory of the strength and security his body had offered as she'd slept against his shoulder drifted disturbingly across Claudia's mind, and she pushed it away. So what if he had let her lean against him? It was true, too, that he had been quite comforting when the engine failed, but the rest of the time he had been rude and critical and generally thoroughly disagreeable, and she disliked him intensely.

So why did the thought of sleeping next to him bother her so much?

'Perhaps I could sleep in the car,' she offered hesitantly to his back. 'I could tell Amil that we had a row.'

David sighed. 'I think you've made up enough stories,' he said, turning off the straining tap and splashing his face and chest with water. 'You've done quite enough damage as it is.'

'What do you mean?'

'I had an interesting little chat with Amil while you were asleep,' he said. He began lathering soap. 'It turns out that he's Sheikh Saïd's nephew.'

'Oh?' said Claudia, too concerned with the prospect of sharing a bed to be very much interested in Amil's family connections. 'What a coincidence.'

'Isn't it?' said David, soaping himself vigorously. 'He'll be able to take us right to the door.'

Claudia could see that some sort of response was required, but she didn't see what he was getting at. 'So?'

'So I'm not going to be able to dump you off with Lucy as soon as we get there.' Rinsing off the soap, David reached for a towel and turned to regard Claudia with a sardonic eye.

'Why not?' she said blankly.

'Because,' he said as he towelled his chest and arms, 'you and I are going to have to stay "married" as long as we're in Telama'an.'

Claudia stared at him. *'What?'*

'You heard,' said David grimly. 'You told Amil that you were my wife, and now you're going to have to stay that way.'

CHAPTER FOUR

'*BUT*...but that's ridiculous!' Claudia stuttered. 'Why do we need to do that?'

'Use your head,' David said irritably. 'The sheikh's invited me to stay in the guest quarters at his palace, and Amil's going to introduce us as a couple. What's he going to think if you disappear as soon as we arrive?'

'I'm sure we could think of something to tell him,' Claudia tried with an edge of desperation. 'We could say that Lucy was sick or—'

'Believe me, I tried everything,' David interrupted her, throwing his towel over the end of the bed. 'I don't want to carry on with this stupid pretence any more than you do! I did my best to convince Amil that it would be better if you stayed with your cousin, but he wouldn't hear of it. We are both to be his uncle's honoured guests, and that's an end to it.'

'But I can't spend the next two weeks pretending to be your wife!'

'You're going to have to,' he said unsympathetically.

'But...but...' Claudia was incoherent with disbelief at the casual way all her plans had been hijacked. 'But Lucy's expecting me!' she managed at last. 'It'll ruin my whole holiday if I have to spend it with you!'

'Frankly, Claudia, I don't give a damn about your holiday!' said David, exasperated. 'The future of GKS Engineering and the whole project at Telama'an is on the line here. Sheikh Saïd is a difficult man. He can be charming, but he's got a very strong sense of family and he's quick to take offence. If he gets wind of the fact that you and I lied about our marriage just to get a lift

60

from his nephew, he'll understand that we didn't trust Amil.'

He paused. Claudia's face was mutinous and she was obviously not going to be co-operative. David's lips thinned. If it wasn't for her, they wouldn't be in this mess! The least she could do was try and understand his position.

'Look,' he went on, trying to sound reasonable, 'I've spent the last two years building up a good relationship with the sheikh. The fact that he's invited me to stay with him suggests that he's planning to give us the contract for the next phase, but nothing is signed yet and we've still got to get through a series of meetings. If he's well-disposed towards me, everything will go well, but he's more than capable of turning round and awarding the contract to another firm if he's displeased. I haven't got this far just to chuck everything in so you can spend your holiday pursuing some mythical destiny with Justin Darke!'

Why, why, why had she ever mentioned that stupid prediction? Claudia stared at David in frustration. It had seemed such a good joke at the time to let him think that she was silly enough to set off in search of a perfect stranger just because of something someone had said at a fête years before, but she had obviously been a little too convincing.

'I've got no intention of pursuing anybody,' she tried, but David only sneered.

'Oh, yes, you're going to leave it up to destiny, aren't you? Well, destiny either has a sense of humour or a rotten sense of timing. As far as I'm concerned Justin is welcome to you, but *I'm* the unfortunate man who's lumbered with you for the next two weeks!'

How could she explain now that she had just been joking? 'Look, all I really want to do is spend my holiday with my cousin,' said Claudia helplessly. 'I really don't care about anything else at the moment.'

'You can do that just as well pretending to be my wife,' he pointed out. 'The sheikh's guest quarters are pretty much like a hotel and you're free to come and go as you please most of the time. I'm going to be involved in meetings, so nobody will be surprised if you spend your days with Lucy.'

'It's not the days I'm worried about,' said Claudia with something of a snap.

'I'm not planning any long nights making mad, passionate love to you if that's what you're afraid of,' he sneered.

She eyed him with dislike. 'The thought never crossed my mind,' she said coldly.

'Then what's the problem?'

'The problem is that I've had the worst year of my life, and all I wanted was to get away. And now that I've *got* away I'm going to have to waste my precious two-week holiday pretending to be married to the most arrogant, unpleasant man I've ever had the misfortune to meet! On top of that, I'm facing the prospect of hurtling into middle age tomorrow in your company, instead of spending my birthday with friends! Isn't that enough of a problem for you?'

David looked exasperated. 'Why do you keep harping on about turning thirty?' he demanded. 'It's no different from any other age.'

'It will be for me,' she said sullenly. 'I'm going to have a crisis, and I don't want to have it with you!'

'In that case, you'll have to pull yourself together, won't you?' he said, unmoved. 'I'm sure I don't need to remind you that it was your idea. I'm not exactly ecstatic at the prospect of spending the next fortnight with the silliest, most exasperating woman *I've* ever met!' he added with brutal candour. 'Unfortunately, it's too late to change things now. As far as everyone else in Telama'an is concerned, we're married until I can put you on a plane out of the country. Believe me, that moment can't come soon enough for me, but until then we're just going to have to make the best of it.'

'And what if I simply refuse to act as your wife any longer?' Claudia tilted her chin belligerently. 'I could tell Amil the truth tomorrow morning. I'm sure he wouldn't abandon us here.'

'You could do that,' David agreed pleasantly. 'And I could tell Justin Darke just what you're doing out here, couldn't I?'

Winter-grey eyes clashed with smoke-grey as they locked gazes. Claudia longed to tell him that he could say what he chose, but it might be extremely embarrassing for Lucy and the unknown Justin, let alone for *her*, if David spread it around that she had flown out on such a ridiculous errand. She knew how rumours worked, and nobody would ever quite believe that she had been joking.

She knew, too, that the whole stupid situation was her own fault. She couldn't really blame it on David. Telling Amil that she was married had seemed such a brilliant idea at the time, and look where it had got her!

Suddenly overwhelmed by a sense of defeat, she dropped her eyes and slumped back down into the chair. 'I don't believe this,' she said, tired, querulous and on the verge of tears. 'I wish I'd never heard of this stupid country! First the plane is delayed, then it almost crashes, then it's a choice between spending two days in a dump in the middle of the desert or being jolted around in the most uncomfortable vehicle I've travelled in, and now *this*! Turning thirty in the middle of nowhere and wasting my entire holiday pretending to be married when all I wanted was a good time!'

David looked at her slumped in the chair, her blonde

hair pushed despairingly behind her ears and her face screwed up with the effort of not crying. He couldn't decide whether he wanted to put her over his knee and spank her, or gather her into his arms and tell her that everything would be all right.

He compromised in the end with brusque understanding. 'Look, let's leave it. We're both tired, and maybe things won't seem so bad in the morning. Why don't you have a wash and then we can try and get some sleep?'

'I suppose so.' Claudia nodded dully, exhaustion rolling over her like a wave. She wasn't sure she could even get up off the chair, let alone get ready for bed.

In the end it was David who filled the basin for her, found a towel and handed her her bag. Moving like an automaton, Claudia took off her make-up, washed her face, cleaned her teeth, and ventured down the corridor to a dark, noisome lavatory. By the time she got back, she had recovered sufficiently to remember her qualms about the most difficult bit: getting into bed with David.

He was stretched out on the bed when she came in, legs crossed and arms beneath his head. He watched with an ironic expression as Claudia pointedly turned her back and pulled on a baggy T-shirt before wriggling with difficulty out of her bra and into clean knickers. It was stuffy in the little room, and she didn't think she could bear to wear anything else, but at least she was decent.

David had obviously considered that keeping his trousers on was enough to preserve the decencies, but his bare chest was unnerving. Claudia wondered if she could ask him to put a shirt on, but didn't want him to know that it bothered her.

It *didn't* bother her, she told herself firmly. After all, wasn't she going to be thirty the next day? She was supposed to be on the verge of becoming a mature, sophisticated woman who could deal with any situation.

She wasn't going to be thrown into a tizzy by a man's chest, for heaven's sake!

Taking a deep breath, she turned. David wondered if she knew how much more appealing she looked with her face bare, tucking her hair behind her ears in an unconsciously nervous gesture. Her legs seemed to go on for ever beneath the T-shirt, and, as if suddenly aware of how much thigh it exposed, she tugged at the hem in a futile attempt to make it a bit longer.

'Shall I turn the light out?' she asked quickly.

David too thought it would be easier in the dark.

He waited as she crossed to the door and pulled the switch. The room was plunged into blackness and she had to feel her way back towards the bed, trying not to think about the cockroaches. Her foot touched something metal, and she put out a hand, only to encounter firm male flesh beneath her fingers.

Whipping her hand back with a muttered apology, she hesitated. Now what? Was she supposed to just jump in next to him? It was all very well being mature and sophisticated, but how did mature and sophisticated women cope with getting into bed with perfect strangers? Perhaps she would wake up tomorrow on her thirtieth birthday miraculously knowing the answer?

The bed creaked, and she could hear David shifting his weight. 'There's plenty of room,' he said calmly out of the darkness.

Claudia reached down a cautious hand again and this time found mattress. She edged closer. It would be more dignified to sit down on the edge of the bed and then swing her legs up.

Unfortunately, dignity evaporated as soon as something scuttly brushed against her foot. With a muffled shriek, Claudia leapt onto the bed, landing in a scramble of limbs on top of David.

'Ouf!' he gasped, and his arms instinctively went out

to steady her. 'That's the first time a girl has literally jumped into bed with me!'

'It was a choice between you or a cockroach,' said Claudia, flustered by the feel of his warm flesh and trying desperately to disentangle herself.

'I'm flattered!' David sat up, more disturbed by finding her tangled up with him than he wanted to admit. 'Look, stop floundering around. *I'll* get off and brave the cockroach.' He swung his legs onto the floor. 'Right, now you lie down.'

Somewhat reassured by his prosaic, not to say brusque attitude, Claudia did as she was told, tugging down her T-shirt which had ridden up disastrously and turning onto her side so that she could cling to the side of the bed. David didn't sound in the least like a man who had seduction on his mind, but it didn't stop her tensing and clutching at the edge of the mattress as it sagged with his weight.

'Relax,' he said irritably as he settled his lean length beside her. The bed was so narrow that it was impossible not to touch each other. He tried to turn away from her so that they were back to back, but he ended up hanging halfway out of the bed. 'This is ridiculous,' he muttered, and rolled over so that they lay like spoons, Claudia's back curled into the shelter of his body and his arm over her. 'There, that's better. At least I'm not trying to sleep suspended in mid-air now.' He shifted slightly. 'Comfortable?' he asked Claudia.

'Oh, *yes*, of course.' Sarcasm was the best refuge against a disturbing awareness of the body lying so close to hers. 'I'm squeezed onto two inches of a lumpy, flea-ridden mattress with a man I only met for the first time this morning. How could I not be comfortable?'

'Things could be worse,' he pointed out with hateful reasonableness.

'How?' said Claudia grumpily.

'You could still be sitting on those orange plastic chairs at Al Mishrah, for a start.'

'There's that, I suppose,' she allowed grudgingly, but it didn't really help her to ignore the hard strength of David's body lying against hers. Her spine registered each rise and fall of his chest, and she could just feel the hairs on his forearm where it rested just below her bare arm. If she moved her hand just a fraction, she could run her fingers over them, and the thought made her shiver with inexplicable temptation.

David felt the slim body quiver and he sighed. 'You can stop tensing every time I move,' he told her in a resigned voice. 'I'm not going to pounce on you. Quite apart from anything else, I'm dog-tired. If I move my arm, it's because I'm trying to get comfortable, not because I'm about to make a grab for you, all right?'

'All right,' she mumbled, feeling foolish.

'Let's try and get some sleep, then,' said David. 'Tomorrow's going to be a long day.'

Sleep? *Sleep?* How could she possibly sleep when her heart was booming, and her body burning with awareness? Claudia lay rigidly, listening to his slow, steady breathing, resenting his ability to relax so utterly. He might as well have been sharing the bed with an oddly shaped bolster for all the notice he took of her. His lack of interest ought to have been reassuring, but somehow Claudia found herself wishing that he had been a little more embarrassed at the situation. Anyone would think he slept with strange women every night.

Perhaps he did, she thought, and a tiny sigh escaped her. She didn't know why, but the idea was oddly depressing.

The beep of the alarm on his watch dragged David up from fathomless sleep. Forcing open one eye, he squinted blearily at the luminous dial: five o'clock. It was still dark, and he gave a deep sigh, too asleep to remember where he was or why he had set the alarm for such an unearthly hour.

Succumbing to the pull of exhaustion, David buried his face back into the silky hair and breathed in the warm fragrance of a sleeping woman's skin. Almost subconsciously, he registered the soft body that was relaxed into the curve of his body, and without thinking what he was doing he tightened his arm around her and nuzzled a sleepy kiss into her neck.

Claudia stirred sleepily, surfacing to a feeling of utter comfort and security. A strong arm was around her, holding her close against a wonderfully hard body. Instinctively, she turned into it and snuggled closer to mumble an endearment into the warm skin of his throat before drifting little kisses towards his jaw.

Lost in a limbo between sleep and wakefulness, it all seemed quite natural to David and it never occurred to him to question what was happening. All that mattered were her lips, teasing up his throat, and the warm, inviting body pressed against his.

Gathering her closer, he kissed her hair, her temple, her eyes and then found her mouth seeking his. Adrift in unreality, they exchanged soft, tender kisses that drew them deliciously out of sleep. Claudia surfaced into hazy delight and she twined her arms around his neck, abandoning herself to the sheer pleasure of the lips exploring hers with such seductive skill.

The movement of her body awoke an instant response in David, and as their kisses deepened he eased her beneath him, letting his hand slide possessively up the smooth length of her thigh, rucking up the T-shirt, curving over her hip and around her breast with increasing urgency. Claudia murmured deep in her throat and her fingers dug into his back as she arched in unspoken invitation.

Whispering endearments against satiny skin, David began to kiss his way downwards. He was intoxicated by her sweetness, by the eager pliancy of the slender body, and he felt tenderness dissolve into desire as he pressed her down into the mattress, his mouth insistent and his hands—

'David? Claudia? Are you awake?'

The voice calling through the door broke through the sense of bewitching unreality that had them both in thrall, and they both froze, David's lips warm against Claudia's throat, and her fingers tangled pleadingly in his hair.

'Claudia?' David echoed, completely disorientated, just as Claudia whispered faintly, disbelievingly,

'David?'

Reality, memory, appalled realisation hit them both at the same time and they jerked apart in horror, too shocked at first to do anything other than stare at each other through the darkness.

'It's after five o'clock!' Amil tried again, pitching his voice higher, and this time David forced his numb mind to react.

'We're awake. We'll be with you in a minute.' His voice sounded creaky and strange, but Amil seemed to be satisfied to hear any sign of life.

'There is breakfast when you are ready,' he called, and moved off.

For a long moment, neither moved. Then David swore under his breath and swung his legs to the floor, dropping his head between his hands as he sat on the side of the bed and fought the arousal still beating through his body.

'What a way to wake up!' he managed at last, drawing a ragged breath.

'Wh-what happened?' If anything Claudia sounded even more disorientated than he felt.

'I must have been half asleep,' said David, as if to himself. 'I woke up and there was someone there and suddenly...' He trailed off, unable to explain how utterly natural it had seemed. After a moment, he lifted his head and glanced at Claudia, who still lay stunned against the pillow. 'I'm sorry,' he said with difficulty. 'I didn't realise it was you.'

'I thought...I thought...' No more than David could Claudia explain what she had thought. She hadn't been thinking at all; that was the trouble.

'I know,' he said. 'I don't think either of us knew what we were doing.'

Claudia moistened her lips. 'No,' she said unsteadily. She still couldn't quite adjust to the abrupt transition to reality. Her mind knew that it was five o'clock and that Amil had interrupted them in the nick of time, but her body wanted to be back in the dream where the only reality was the swirl of enchanted sensation. God only knew what would have happened if Amil hadn't knocked just then!

Well, she knew too. It was perfectly obvious what would have happened. Claudia turned her face into the pillow and tried not to think about how right it had felt, tried not to wish that Amil hadn't knocked just when he had. Her skin twitched and tingled where he had touched her, and she lifted a hand to cover her mouth as if she could still feel his stubble grazing her face.

David got up in an abrupt movement and switched on the light before splashing cold water over his head. He towelled himself dry with unnecessary roughness and pulled a clean shirt from his case. Only then did he turn and look at Claudia.

She was huddled on the bed, her eyes huge and dazed. 'Are you all right?' he asked gruffly as he fastened the buttons on his shirt with hands that were still not quite steady.

'Yes.' Her eyes slid away from his. 'Yes, I'm fine.'

'I'll go and have a word with Amil,' he said a little uncertainly, thinking that if she had had half the shock he had she might need some time on her own to recover. 'Don't be too long.'

Claudia's legs trembled so violently when she tried to stand up that she had to hang onto the bed. Somehow she managed to wash her face, but her hand was too unsteady to put on any mascara and in the end she just combed her hair. Sitting on the edge of the bed, she peered at herself in the mirror and grimaced at her reflection as she remembered that it was her thirtieth birthday. She had been supposed to wake up this morning a changed woman, mature, confident, in control—not moaning with pleasure in the arms of a man who didn't even realise who she was!

Claudia burned remembering the look of dismay on David's face. Who had he *thought* he was kissing? She snapped the mirror shut and stood up. Her instinct was to curl up in a tiny ball and hide herself in the corner, but she was awake now, and she knew that she would have to face him again.

After all, they had both made fools of themselves. There was nothing to make a fuss about. If David expected her to make a big deal of waking up with him like that, then he would be in for a surprise. No, she would be cool and calm and impress him with her mature dismissal of the whole affair, and then there would be not the slightest chance of him suspecting that his touch had had the slightest effect on her anyway.

Well, it hadn't, Claudia told herself as she dressed in jeans and a soft blue shirt, the plainest and least revealing outfit she could find. God forbid that David should think that she was interested in *him*! Her mind shied away from memories of the tender kisses she and David had shared, the slow sear of passion and the aching excitement of his hands sliding over her skin. She had thought he was Michael, that was all.

Deep inside Claudia, a voice pointed out that Michael had never, ever kissed her like that, but she scowled and quashed it firmly. It was her birthday, and she could lie to herself if she wanted to.

The muezzin was calling the faithful to prayer as they drove into Telama'an twelve long, hot, joltingly uncomfortable hours later. They had left Sifa as the sky flushed with dawn, and now the sun was sinking once more, washing the flat-roofed houses and narrow streets of the oasis in a hushed, unearthly light.

The palace itself was set in a grove of date palms outside the town. To Claudia's relief, they were shown straight to the guest quarters, a self-contained unit a little distance from the palace itself, and built around a shady courtyard where water from a fountain trickled into a small pool. There was a luxuriously appointed bathroom, a sitting area, and a bedroom—with just one, wide bed.

'Well,' said Claudia, averting her eyes from the bedroom door and wandering nervously out to inspect the pool.

'Well,' David agreed somewhat sardonically. 'You seem to have survived the crisis of turning thirty, anyway.'

She gave a mirthless laugh. 'It certainly hasn't felt much like a birthday, so far.'

'I'm afraid Sifa wasn't the ideal place to pop out and find you a card,' he said. 'But I apologise for not wishing you a happy birthday this morning. I had other things on my mind when I woke up.'

Claudia's cheeks burned at his casual reference to that morning. She had managed to get through the whole day without meeting David's eyes once, but it hadn't stopped her being agonisingly aware of him. No matter how hard she'd braced her hand against the dashboard, every bump, every lurch of the truck had tipped them together and every time her nerves had exploded with the remembered touch of his body.

She had longed for the terrible journey to be over, but now that it was she felt if anything even more uncomfortable than she had wedged into the front of the pick-up truck for twelve hours. With never-failing courtesy, Amil had escorted them to the guest quarters, and waved aside their attempts to thank him for everything he had done. 'My uncle will see you tomorrow,' he said, 'when you have had a chance to rest.' He'd pointed out a Jeep sitting under a tree. 'That vehicle is at your disposal. Please use it whenever you like. Otherwise, if there is anything you need, just ring the bell and someone will come.'

Claudia wondered if she could ring the bell and ask to have her memory wiped, or, better still, to have time rewound to five o'clock that morning so that she could start the day rather differently. Instead of turning and snuggling into David's arms, she would push him briskly aside and jump out of bed, and the ghastly tension between them now wouldn't exist.

She eyed David resentfully from under her lashes. Couldn't he feel the very air strumming with the memory of that kiss? How could he *joke* about it? Other things on his mind indeed! He obviously wasn't thinking about them now as he dropped into a chair and rubbed a hand over his face in a tired gesture. 'I need a shave,' he said, closing his eyes with a sigh. 'God, what a trip!'

Claudia was seized by an entirely unexpected and disconcerting urge to go over and massage the tiredness from his neck and shoulders. Fortunately, it was immediately contradicted by the need to prove to him beyond question that she was treating that morning's kiss as lightly as he was. She might not be able to manage an equally sarcastic comment, but she could certainly show him that she too had other things on her mind now, and they were a lot more important than a shave!

Turning, she hoisted her case onto the bed and snapped it open. 'I'll just have a shower and then I'll go,' she said.

David opened his eyes. 'Go where?' he asked, his voice ominously quiet.

'To Lucy's, of course.'

'Now?'

'Why not?'

'Claudia, you've been travelling for over twelve hours,' he pointed out wearily. 'Can't you wait until to-morrow?'

She turned to him, eyes wide with mock consternation. 'How could you have forgotten?' she accused him, and pressed a hand to her throat to indicate emotion. 'I have to meet ''JD'' on my thirtieth birthday or I'll miss my destiny!'

David covered his eyes with his hand. 'Oh, God, not that again! You don't think if destiny's going to go to so much trouble it would allow you to be a day late?'

'But David, it doesn't work like that,' Claudia said, rather pleased with the note of throaty sincerity in her voice. 'I just have to meet JD—whoever he is—tonight, and I'm not going to meet him here, am I?'

'I'm certainly not going to hold a party just so you can review every man for the right initials,' snapped David. 'What makes you so certain that Justin will be at Lucy's tonight, anyway?'

'*I* didn't say I was going to meet Justin Darke. If JD isn't at Lucy's...well, destiny must have something else in mind, but at least I'll have done everything I can.'

David sighed and hauled himself to his feet. 'I don't think I'll pay you the compliment of logical argument,' he said caustically. 'If you're so determined to go, we'd better get going. You've only got—' he made a pretence at looking at his watch '—three and a half hours to meet your destiny!'

We? Claudia looked at him in consternation. 'You don't need to come!'

'How else do you propose to get to Lucy's?'

'Can't I get a taxi?'

'Lucy lives on a compound five miles away. You won't get a taxi to take you there at this time of night.'

'Well, I could take the car,' she said, determined not to be beaten. She didn't want David muscling in on her reunion with Lucy and Patrick. She didn't want David anywhere near her until she could forget that kiss and treat him with the same disinterest as he was treating her. 'Amil said we could use it.'

'Amil said *I* could use it. Women don't drive in Shofrar.'

'How ridiculous!' said Claudia, tossing her hair angrily.

'I dare say it is,' David said evenly, 'but it's the custom here, and it's not your place to criticise how the Shofranis choose to run their own affairs.'

'In that case, I'll ring Lucy and ask Patrick to come and get me.'

David pinched the bridge of his nose. 'There's no need to do that. I've already said that I'll take you.'

'But you don't want to come,' she objected.

'I don't want to sit here looking a fool while my so-called wife swans off into the night on our first evening either,' he snapped. 'I need to see Patrick anyway to explain about this farce that I seem to have ended up in, and if you insist on going tonight I don't have much choice but to go with you. I'm not staying long, though,' he warned. 'So if you want to have a shower before you go you'd better get a move on.'

A few minutes later Claudia stood under the streaming

water and told herself that she wasn't going to let
David's kiss bother her. It was just a kiss, after all, and
now that she was thirty she ought to be beyond getting
into a state about someone who had kissed her without
even knowing who she was. David appeared to have
shrugged off the whole incident and so would she.

At least, she would try. A long, slow shiver ran down
Claudia's spine. The feel of David's hands still lingered
on her skin, the taste of his mouth still tingled on her
lips, but she would die rather than let him guess that she
remembered it so clearly. If he did, he would only think
that she was interested in *him*, and Claudia's pride
bristled at the very idea.

No, let David believe that her heart was set on Justin
Darke. Let him realise how little she cared *what* he
thought of her. She was *not* going to let him spoil her
time in Shofrar! When Claudia thought of how she had
had to grovel to her boss to get this fortnight off, her
chin tilted at a stubborn angle that David would already
have recognised as familiar. This was her holiday, and
she was going to have a good time, David Stirling or no
David Stirling!

CHAPTER FIVE

'CLAUDIA!'

'Lucy!' The cousins fell into each other's arms, hugging with excitement.

'You made it!' shrieked Lucy. 'I knew you would! Happy birthday!' She embraced her cousin again until she suddenly caught sight of David, waiting behind Claudia with a resigned expression. *'David!'* she exclaimed in astonishment. 'What on earth are you doing here?'

'It's a very long story,' he said dryly. 'Isn't it, Claudia?'

'We were on the same plane,' Claudia explained, thinking it would be as well to start with the easy bit. 'I suppose you heard about the delay?'

'They said you wouldn't get here for another two days,' said Lucy. 'But I knew you wouldn't let a little thing like engine failure stop you! How did you get here, anyway?'

'Well, er, it's a bit complicated,' said Claudia, very conscious of David standing, saturnine, behind her.

'Well, come in first and you can tell us when we've cracked open the champagne!' Lucy held the door wide open and called inside. 'Patrick! Look who it is!'

A squarely built man with a pleasant face and twinkling eyes appeared at the door, and his expression lit up when he saw Claudia. 'Well, well, if it isn't the birthday girl!' He had picked her up in a bear hug that was enormously comforting before he saw David and, like his wife, did a double-take.

'Claudia is going to explain what I'm doing here,' said

David after the two men had shaken hands. The glance he sent Claudia was full of malicious amusement. 'She's going to explain everything.'

'That sounds ominous,' said Patrick lightly. 'You'd better come in and confess, Claudia!'

As they went into the house, Claudia caught Lucy by the arm and pulled her back. 'Can you invite Justin Darke round?' she whispered.

Lucy was plainly startled. 'What, now?'

'I want to meet him tonight,' hissed Claudia, checking that David and Patrick were safely out of earshot. 'Can't you ask him for a drink to celebrate my arrival or something?'

'I could, yes, but wouldn't you rather wait until tomorrow? You must be exhausted.'

'No, it has to be tonight,' she said urgently.

Lucy looked deeply suspicious. 'What's all this about?'

'I can't explain now,' said Claudia, with another furtive glance over her shoulder, 'but it's important, and David mustn't know that I asked you to ask Justin. *Please*, Lucy!'

'OK.' Mystified, but willing to indulge her cousin on her birthday, Lucy disappeared to ring from another room while Claudia joined the men with a bright smile. By the time Patrick had opened the champagne and finished pouring the glasses, Lucy was back.

Catching a glimpse of her cousin's discreet thumbs-up sign, Claudia relaxed. She wasn't quite sure why it was so desperately important to make David believe that she wasn't the slightest bit interested in him when she wasn't, but appearing to be obsessed with another man would surely convince him just in case the idea *should* cross his mind.

She cast David a resentful glance as Patrick handed her a glass. If he hadn't insisted on coming with her tonight, she could have been mysterious and enigmatic when he asked her about her supposed destiny, and simply pretended that she had met a man with the right initials. As it was, she was going to have to drag the unfortunate Justin Darke into the scenario and waste the entire evening making sure David knew that she was interested in *him* instead of relaxing and having a good time with Lucy and Patrick. It wasn't fair and it was all David's fault!

So disgruntled did she feel that when Patrick asked her what she had been up to her reply was very close to a snap. 'It's perfectly simple,' she said. 'The plane broke down and we had a choice of hanging around in Al Mishrah or accepting a lift down here, so I took the lift.'

'And?' David prompted.

Claudia met his sardonic look with an angry shake of her hair. 'And it didn't seem sensible to drive off into the desert on my own with a man I had never met before,' she went on, pointedly addressing herself to Lucy and Patrick. 'I happened to know that David needed to get here as soon as possible, so thought it would be a good idea if we went together.'

'Yes?' Lucy encouraged when Claudia's story faltered. She and Patrick were sitting side by side, gamely trying to understand what the point of the story was.

Claudia, discovering that it wasn't quite as easy to explain as she had thought it would be, glanced at David, but if she had hoped that he might help her out she was doomed to disappointment. He just sat there looking blandly back at her, with only a faint ironic twist to his mouth. She drew a deep breath and turned back to her cousin.

'And so I told Amil that David and I were married,' she finished in a rush, wincing as she saw Lucy's jaw drop. Patrick was looking aghast, which was even worse. 'It just seemed the obvious thing to do at the time,' she said defiantly. 'And I do think David could be more grateful. If it wasn't for me, he could still be sitting in Al Mishrah waiting for a plane!'

'Claudia knows that my gratitude at the casual way she appropriated me as her husband has been rather tempered by the discovery that the man who so kindly drove us down here is a nephew of Sheikh Saïd,' said David in a blistering voice. 'Now Amil has told his uncle that his English guest has arrived with an unexpected wife, who is now generously included in the invitation to stay in the guest quarters. This means that I can't suddenly dispose of my supposed wife tonight, much as I would like to.'

He looked at Claudia, who was sitting bolt upright on the sofa, flushed with defiance, pale gold hair pushed crossly behind her ears. 'I'm sorry if I don't seem very *grateful*,' he said, 'but frankly I've got more important matters on my mind. I could do without being saddled with a wife at the best of times, but I sure as hell don't need one when I'm trying to concentrate on the contracts, and I *certainly* don't need one like you!'

'Then why can't I just come and stay with Lucy and Patrick as I planned?' Claudia's chin was set at a mutinous angle. 'I can't see that this sheikh person is going to care one way or the other. He probably won't know if I'm there or not.'

'Oh, he will,' said Patrick seriously. 'Saïd knows exactly what's going on, inside and outside his palace. I'm afraid you can't come here, Claudia. The sheikh's good opinion is vital to us at the moment and he would be very offended if you seemed to spurn his hospitality.' He rubbed his jaw in concern. 'I'm sorry about this, David. It's obviously put you in an extremely difficult position.'

Claudia looked at Patrick in disgust. 'Why are you apologising to *him*?' she demanded indignantly before

David could answer. 'What about the difficult position *I'm* in?'

'Well...' Patrick hesitated. 'It does rather sound as if it was your idea,' he excused himself.

'It wasn't my idea to spend my holiday married to Mr Grumpy!' snapped Claudia. 'Why can't you just send him back to London, Patrick? Tell the sheikh that some crisis has come up and that David has to leave, but that since I've come all this way it seems a pity for me not to spend some time with my cousin, so I'm going to stay?' She looked around, pleased with her idea. 'It would solve all our problems. David can give you all his papers and you can deal with these stupid negotiations—I'm sure you'd do a better job!' she added, with a nasty look sideways to where David was sitting watching her with a profoundly irritated expression.

'That's a good idea, Claudia,' said Patrick, obviously picking his words with care. 'There is just one tiny problem, though. I'm afraid I'm not in a position to send David anywhere.'

'Why not? You're the senior engineer out here, aren't you?'

'Yes,' he agreed, 'but I work for GKS Engineering Associates. Do you know what those letters stand for, Claudia?'

What was he going on about? 'GKS?' she said impatiently. 'No.'

'They stand for Greville, Keen and Stirling,' said Patrick. 'That's Stirling as in David Stirling. Greville and Keen retired a long time ago, and now David *is* GKS Engineering—and that makes him the one that gives the orders, not me.'

There was a moment of utter silence before Claudia turned accusingly to David. 'You're Patrick's boss?'

'I don't usually describe myself in that way, but, yes, I am.'

'Why didn't you tell me?'

He shrugged. 'It never seemed appropriate.'

'Really?' she said with withering sarcasm. 'You don't think it might perhaps have been appropriate to have told me when I was threatening to tell Patrick to sack you?' Patrick covered his eyes with his hand and Lucy smothered a nervous giggle, but Claudia ignored them both. 'You let me make a fool of myself!'

'You didn't need any encouragement from me!' snapped David.

Claudia opened her mouth to retort, but Lucy got in first. 'Um… Claudia?' she said with mock hesitation. 'Patrick and I are on your side—*of course*—but Patrick *does* have quite a good job, and we'd both like to stay here in Telama'an, so we'd really, really appreciate it if you could just try and be nice to David!'

'I don't see why I should,' said Claudia belligerently. 'He's not nice to me! And if he's the type of man who would sack Patrick just because of something I said Patrick wouldn't want to work for him anyway!'

'Of course I'm not going to sack Patrick,' David said, annoyed at the very suggestion. He glowered at Claudia, who glared back at him. Her cheeks were flushed, her eyes glittering, and that chin was tilted at a dangerous angle.

Had he really only known her for a day and a half? It hardly seemed possible to imagine a time when she hadn't been an irritation, a distraction, an enormous complication in his well-ordered life.

He let out an abrupt, exasperated breath. 'Look, let's call a truce,' he said after a moment. 'What's done is done. We both wanted to get here, and now we're both here, and I am certainly not going to jeopardise the future of my firm by cancelling my meetings with the sheikh and sloping back to London just so that you can enjoy your holiday!

'Neither of us wants to have to pretend to be married for any longer than is necessary, but I'm afraid there's nothing we can do about it now, so it might be easier if we agreed to at least try and be pleasant to each other. I've got important negotiations to deal with and I don't want to be distracted by silly squabbles any more than you want to waste your holiday arguing.'

'I suppose not,' said Claudia grudgingly.

'So, let's agree on a story about how we came to be married. I don't suppose anyone is going to cross-question us, but there's bound to be some interest.'

'Do all the GKS staff have to think that you're married as well?' asked Lucy.

'Of course they do.' Patrick answered for David. 'You know how everybody gossips. Just because you don't see the sheikh very often, you think that he doesn't know what goes on out here. There are Shofrani staff in the office and at the club: they gossip too, and I'll bet it all filters back to the sheikh eventually. If Claudia and David suddenly stop acting as a couple whenever they come out here, the word will get back to him in no time.'

'But everyone knows that I invited Claudia out here to stay for her birthday,' Lucy objected. 'They were all coming to the party this evening, until we had to cancel it when the plane didn't arrive.'

David frowned. 'Yes, it's a pity about that.' He thought for a minute and then shrugged. 'We'll just have to say that Claudia and I met and got married on the spur of the moment last week, and pass it off as coincidence that she's your cousin.'

'It's not very convincing, though, is it?' Claudia said, dissatisfied. 'I mean, why would we have got married when we hardly knew each other?'

'Haven't you ever heard of falling in love at first sight?'

The irony in David's voice deepened the flush in her

cheeks. 'I've heard of it, but I've never met anyone who actually did it!'

'Well, for the purposes of the next two weeks, you and I no sooner clapped eyes on each other than we fell madly in love. I realise that the whole story is unlikely in the extreme, but it's the best I can do right now.'

'Why didn't I ring Lucy and Patrick to let them know about this amazing coincidence?' she asked.

David glanced at his senior engineer. 'We wanted to surprise them,' he suggested.

'You've certainly done that,' said Patrick with feeling.

'Well,' said Lucy briskly. 'Now that we've sorted all that out, perhaps we can get on with celebrating Claudia's birthday? Come on, Claudia, how does it feel to be thirty?'

Claudia opened her mouth to answer, but before she could speak there was a knock at the door, and she shot a triumphant glance at David. 'It feels great,' she said as Patrick went to the door. 'I've got this wonderful feeling that my life is about to change completely.'

'Really?' said Lucy, impressed.

'Absolutely,' said Claudia, with another peek at David. 'I feel as if my destiny could walk through the door at any moment.'

Right on cue, Justin Darke appeared with Patrick. He was, as Lucy had promised, deliciously attractive, with dark curly hair, warm brown eyes and the kind of smile that would normally have made Claudia go weak at the knees. As it was, she was too busy trying to gauge David's reaction to the apparent fulfillment of her prediction to take in many details about the American.

Behind Justin's back, Patrick was signalling agonised questions to his wife. 'Justin, how nice of you to come,' said Lucy, rising to the occasion. 'We had to cancel tonight's party when the plane was delayed, but Claudia's turned up unexpectedly after all, so I thought it would be nice to have a bit of a celebration for her birthday. Four just doesn't seem enough, so we need you to turn it into a party!'

It was obvious that Justin was more than a little puzzled to find himself the only guest honoured with an invitation to celebrate the arrival of Lucy's cousin, and his baffled look deepened when he saw David Stirling standing there. He had had little to do with the chief executive since he had joined GKS, but all his colleagues spoke of their employer with respect bordering on awe, and Justin was careful to greet him with due deference.

When Patrick explained that David and Claudia had just announced their marriage, Justin was even more surprised, but he congratulated them both warmly. 'Hey, that's great news!' he said, shaking David's hand. 'But I don't want to butt in on a family occasion...'

'Oh, don't go!' begged Claudia with a dazzling smile. 'Lucy's right—you can't have a party with just four people, and I've been looking forward to meeting you so much!' Sitting down on the sofa, she patted the place beside her invitingly.

Effectively excluded, David, Lucy and Patrick had little choice but to move together to the opposite side of the room. 'I don't think either of us have thanked you for coming to Claudia's rescue,' said Lucy after a moment. 'I know it's all turned out rather unfortunately, but she was lucky you were there to look after her.'

'I would have said that Claudia was more than capable of looking after herself,' said David with something of a snap. He was trying not to watch her flirting with Justin Darke on the sofa. Really, it was nothing to him if Claudia chose to make a spectacle of herself in pursuit of some poor, unsuspecting male, but did she need to be quite so blatant about it?

'Oh, I know she seems tough,' Lucy was saying, 'but

she's not really. She tries not to show how vulnerable she is, but she's had such a rotten run of luck with men.' She paused, exchanging a look with her husband who was obviously as puzzled as she was by Claudia's uncharacteristic behaviour.

Lucy wished that she knew what was going on. There was Claudia, clearly intent on dazzling Justin on one hand, and David, looking alarmingly saturnine on the other. Were she and Patrick supposed to be distracting him?

'Did Claudia tell you about Michael?' she asked with an edge of desperation.

David's gaze sharpened. 'No,' he said warily.

'She was madly in love with him,' Lucy remembered. 'They were going to get married in the spring, but he dumped her in the middle of January, the week after she'd lost her job. Everything's gone wrong for Claudia this year,' she sighed. 'There was the job, then Michael, then her flat was broken into and somebody ran into the back of her car...most people would have let it get them down, but Claudia's a fighter. She got herself an even better job, and I think she's finally put Michael behind her, but she desperately needed this holiday.'

Lucy hesitated. 'I'm only telling you all this so you'll understand how important it was for Claudia to get here, David. She's not usually as difficult as she's been with you.'

There was an odd feeling in David's chest. He hadn't taken in much more than the fact that Claudia had been desperately in love with someone called Michael. Was that who she had thought he was this morning when she had returned his kisses with such warmth and abandon?

He looked over to where she sat on the sofa, giving Justin Darke the benefit of those amazing eyes. It looked as if she was more than ready to console herself for Michael, he thought dourly. Claudia could talk all she wanted about destiny, but David was prepared to bet that she had known perfectly well that she was going to meet Justin tonight, and she had gone to a lot of trouble to impress the American.

She was wearing some kind of outfit in a deep blue silk, a simple, stylish top with trousers that relied on the sheen of the rich material to suggest a sexiness that a more revealing dress, for instance, would have utterly destroyed. The colour of the silk deepened the blue in her eyes and set off the pale gold hair and the luminous glow of her skin, as Claudia was no doubt well aware.

David watched her laughing with Justin. She looked vibrant, alive, and as she leant forward to pick up her glass the silk smoothed against the outline of her breasts. Assailed by the sudden vivid memory of how her skin had felt beneath his hands that morning, David drew a short, sharp breath and turned abruptly back to Lucy and Patrick. He wasn't about to give Claudia the satisfaction of knowing that the feel of her body lingered distractingly in his mind, or of thinking that he cared in the least why, how or with whom she chose to flaunt herself!

'You don't need to explain anything about Claudia to me,' he said. 'It's really not any of my business. As far as I'm concerned, as long as she doesn't upset the negotiations in any way, she can enjoy her holiday out here with whoever she likes.'

Lucy was more than a little daunted by the coolness in his voice. She had always got on well with David, but she had never seen him look this formidable before and she wasn't quite sure how to respond.

David saw her glance surreptitiously at Patrick and receive a baffled shrug in return, and wished he hadn't sounded quite so quelling. It wasn't fair to take his bad temper out on them. *They* hadn't thrust themselves into his life or turned his plans upside down or ridden roughshod over his feelings, and they weren't involved in that revolting performance on the sofa either.

'I'm sorry.' He apologised to them both with a rueful grin. 'It's been a long day.' With an effort he closed his mind to Claudia and smiled at Lucy instead. 'You always know all the gossip, Lucy. Tell me what's been going on since I was last here.'

From the sofa, Claudia saw his smile and was conscious of a sudden breathlessness. He had never smiled at *her* like that. Come to think of it, he had never smiled at her at all. She hadn't realised how much younger and more approachable he would look, or how the creases deepening in his cheeks and crinkling around his eyes would transform his face from austerity into an almost rakish charm.

Claudia took firm control of her breathing. It was only a smile. It just meant that he was enjoying himself with Lucy and not in the least bothered by the fact that she was talking to a much younger, much more attractive and *much* more charming man. You'd think if she was supposed to be his new bride he would be showing *some* interest in what she was doing, but no! Look at him, smiling at Lucy like that as if she wasn't even there!

Claudia's eyes gleamed a sudden, dangerous shade of blue, and she shook her hair away from her face almost as if accepting a challenge. It was her birthday, she was thirty, and if anyone was going to have a good time it was going to be *her*!

She turned her attention to Justin, who had been politely asking about her trip, and bestowed such a brilliant smile on him that he actually blinked. 'That's enough about that ghastly journey,' she said, pitching her voice slightly higher so that David couldn't avoid hearing her. 'Tell me about *you*.'

She made Justin tell her all about his job, his family, whether he missed the States, what books he read, what music he liked. Justin was clearly taken aback, and not entirely sure how to respond to the new Mrs Stirling's apparent fascination with the lives of her husband's employees. Whenever he tried to steer the subject away from himself and back to more neutral ground, Claudia would determinedly steer it back, although she was finding it a laborious process.

It wasn't that Justin wasn't charming—he was. It was just that it was impossible to concentrate on what he was saying when she kept catching glimpses of David out of the corner of her eye. He was chatting easily with Lucy and Patrick—they were even *laughing* together, she noted bitterly—and if he remembered that she was in the room he gave absolutely no sign of it. How could he realise that she stood in no danger of being attracted to him if he didn't even notice how hard she was working for another man's attention?

All at once, Claudia was overwhelmed by exhaustion. An awareness of how irrationally she was behaving combined with the accumulated tensions of the day and the effects of the bone-rattling journey to roll over her in a wave of tiredness so physical that Claudia's shoulders actually slumped beneath its weight.

'How do you like staying in the sheikh's palace, Mrs Stirling?' Her momentary distraction gave Justin the opportunity to change the conversation. 'I haven't been there, but I hear it's a fabulous place.'

With an enormous effort, Claudia stiffened her spine and fixed her smile back in place. 'Please, call me Claudia,' she insisted. 'Mrs Stirling makes me sound so...'

'Married?' David suggested in a cool voice, appearing suddenly beside the sofa, and his smile held a distinct warning. 'We haven't been married very long,' he explained to Justin, 'and she keeps forgetting. Don't you, darling?' he added, with a faint, mocking stress on that last word.

'How could I forget?' said Claudia sweetly, but David was quick to notice that the challenge in the smoky eyes was dulled for once.

'Come on,' he said almost roughly. 'It's time we went. You're exhausted.'

'I'm fine,' she protested automatically, but it was almost a relief when David reached down an autocratic hand and pulled her to her feet.

His fingers were warm and strong, and Claudia had a crazy impulse to cling to them, to lean into the shelter of his hard body and feel his arm close around her. She must be more tired than she'd thought. Resolutely, she forced herself to drop his hand and step away.

'Do we really have to go now?'

'I must go, too,' said Justin hurriedly.

He left first, disappearing into the night with a wave as Patrick and Lucy accompanied David and Claudia to the car. 'Well,' said Lucy a little too heartily into the momentary silence. 'What did you think of Justin?'

Claudia sensed David stiffen beside her as he opened the door for her. 'Oh, I thought he was *gorgeous*!' she gushed. 'You were right, Lucy, he's everything I've ever wanted in a man. So warm and charming and intelligent.' Encouraged by the muscle twitching at the corner of David's mouth, she heaved a gusty sigh. 'And so *caring*, too. I can't wait to see him again already. You will invite him again, won't you?'

'Er, yes, of course,' said Lucy, completely thrown by Claudia's extravagant reaction. She cast a glance of anguished appeal at Patrick, who came nobly to his wife's rescue.

'Why don't we rearrange Claudia's party for tomorrow night? We'll invite everybody, including Justin.'

'As long as he's there,' said Claudia with a misty

look. At least David didn't look as if he was enjoying himself any more. He had got into the driving seat and was waiting, boot-faced, with his hand on the ignition.

Lucy was also watching David, although with more anxiety. 'Justin's lovely, and I'm glad you like him, of course,' she began hesitantly, 'but it's all a bit awkward, isn't it?'

'What do you mean?'

'What Lucy is trying to say is that Justin believes that you're married to me,' David put in, an unpleasant edge to his voice. 'And as Justin isn't the kind of man to get involved with another man's wife you're not likely to get very far with him.'

'Well, we'll see, won't we?' said Claudia, hugging Lucy goodbye and climbing in beside him. She wound down the window so that she could lean out to her cousin. 'Just make sure Justin comes to the party to-morrow. I've just got a feeling that he's the man for me, and if he is it won't matter about David and this silly marriage business. Destiny will find a way for us to be together!'

'Destiny will find a way!' David mimicked savagely as they drove off. 'Justin's gorgeous!'

'He was,' said Claudia with a defiant toss of her head. 'And after spending the last two days with you I can't tell you what a pleasure it was to meet a man who was attractive and charming and plain nice!'

'You left out *caring*,' snarled David, changing gear with unnecessary force. 'Lucy and Patrick should have provided sick-bags! It was all we could do not to throw up watching you tonight—you were all over him like a rash! I know you're desperate, but you won't get Justin that way—the poor man was obviously terrified. You'd be better off playing hard to get.'

'Thank you for your advice,' she said in a voice that dripped ice, 'but nothing I've seen of you so far has led me to believe that you're any kind of expert on seduction!'

'You don't need to be an expert. You just need to be a man to see that all that breathless attention, all those gooey eyes and tell-me-about-*you*s are guaranteed to make anyone turn and run in the opposite direction. Nobody likes feeling pursued, and if ever I saw a man looking hunted it was Justin Darke sitting next to you on that sofa tonight!'

Still smarting at his description of her as desperate, Claudia scowled out of her window at the passing darkness. 'What do you care, anyway?' she demanded.

'I don't care,' said David loftily. 'But you were supposed to have been behaving as my wife, and you weren't doing a very good job of it. All you did was make me look a complete fool!'

Claudia threw him an angry glance. 'Oh, and what was I *supposed* to have been doing? Blowing you kisses?'

'Don't be ridiculous!' he snapped. 'All you had to do was behave like any normal person meeting someone for the first time. Instead of which, you pin one of my employees into a corner of the sofa and practically offer yourself to him on a plate!'

'I did nothing of the kind,' said Claudia between her teeth, too angry now to remember that was exactly what she had wanted David to think she was doing. 'I was merely enjoying a civilised conversation with Justin. Not that *you* would know what I was doing, anyway. You weren't exactly the model of a loving husband, either, were you? You didn't come near me all evening.'

'You made it more than clear that you wanted to keep Justin all to yourself,' he countered. 'I could hardly come and loom over the sofa while you were talking, could I?'

'You could have made more of an effort,' she said

obstinately. 'But you didn't want to. You were obviously having much too good a time with Lucy and Patrick.'

'We *would* have been having a good time if we hadn't had to listen to your fatuous conversation with Justin,' David snapped back. 'I didn't hear either of you say anything interesting or intelligent all evening, so perhaps you're well matched after all!'

Claudia lifted her chin. 'We are,' she said. If David thought she was really interested in Justin, so much the better. Wasn't that what she wanted? 'We're going to be perfect together.'

CHAPTER SIX

DAVID drove with a kind of cold fury. He didn't know why he felt so angry, but when an inner voice tentatively suggested that he might be jealous he thrust the idea aside in disgust. Jealous of Justin Darke? That would be the day! He was more likely to feel sorry for the American if Claudia really had set her sights on him.

When they got back to the guest quarters, someone had switched on the lamps and turned down the bed. They had preserved a cold silence for the rest of the journey, but once they got inside the anger that had kept them both buoyed up unaccountably dissolved and a new kind of tension closed around them like a fist. All it took was a glimpse of the bed, and the air was vibrating with memories of that morning when they had woken together in another, very different bed.

This was a much wider bed, Claudia tried to reassure herself as she brushed her teeth in the gleaming bathroom. There could hardly have been a greater contrast with last night's cracked basin and clunking taps. *Everything* was different. Both of them had been so horrified that morning that there would be no chance of them making the same mistake again, and anyway, the bed was so wide that they needn't touch at all if they didn't want to.

Which they didn't.

Claudia flicked water off her toothbrush and shut it back in its holder with a snap. There was plenty of room for them both in the bed, and no question of unsolicited advances. David had made it crystal clear that he wasn't attracted to her, that he didn't even like her, so he was hardly likely to come sliding over to her side of the bed, was he?

So why was she thumping with nerves? Why was her blood pounding and her skin strumming and her heart clenching at the very thought of getting into bed beside David again?

If only she could forget how he had kissed her. Claudia could still feel the honeyed sweetness of waking to the warmth of his lips and the glorious sense of rightness as she had turned into his arms. His hands had been so strong and sure, wickedly exciting as they curved over her responsive body, and her fingertips seemed to throb with the memory of his sleek skin...

Horrified by the way her thoughts kept straying into such dangerous areas, Claudia began vigorously rubbing moisturiser into her face and neck. Far better to think about the disgust on David's face when Amil's knock had wrenched them both back to reality. He wouldn't be making the same mistake again, that was for sure.

'Good,' said Claudia out loud to her reflection, and then, when it seemed as if her voice lacked conviction, tried again. 'Very good.'

David was standing out in the courtyard when she came out of the bathroom. His hands were thrust into his pockets and his shoulders were hunched as if against disagreeable thoughts as he stared down at the pool. Claudia looked at his back and for one dangerous moment allowed herself to remember how his muscles had flexed beneath her touch before she wrenched her mind away.

'The bathroom's all yours,' she said coolly.

When he had gone, she changed into the demure T-shirt she had worn the night before and climbed into the bed, pulling the sheet up to her chin. She was thirty, she was mature now, she was cool, she was collected.

She was incredibly, ridiculously nervous.

David came out of the bathroom rubbing his head with a towel. He eyed Claudia lying rigidly beneath the sheet, but made no comment as he cast the towel over a chair and began to unfasten his trousers.

She stiffened. Was he going to climb calmly into bed *naked*? 'I'll keep my shorts on, so there's no need to panic,' he said as if he had read her mind. 'I'm not wearing trousers to bed every night just to satisfy your maidenly scruples. Last night was uncomfortable enough.'

'I couldn't care *less* what you wear,' said Claudia in a frosty voice.

'Good, then you can stop lying there like a sacrificial victim waiting for the knife,' said David, disappearing into the sitting area to click off a lamp there and reappearing in the doorway. 'This bed is wide enough to sleep four in comfort, so we don't even need to brush against each other.'

'I wasn't worried about that,' she lied.

'What were you worried about, then?'

'Nothing,' she said haughtily as he switched off the bedside lamp and pulled back the sheet so that he could lie down.

'Oh, come on, Claudia, you're vibrating like a tuning fork. What is it? Afraid that I might be tempted to take advantage of you?'

Incensed by the mockery in his voice, Claudia bounced up to switch off her own bedside light. 'No,' she said as the room was plunged into darkness. 'But after what happened this morning I might be entitled to be afraid of just that, don't you think?'

'No more than I should be worried that you might take advantage of *me*,' said David with equal coolness.

'Me take advantage of you?' She managed an incredulous laugh. 'That's not very likely, is it?'

'Why not? As I recall it, you were the one who started nuzzling into me this morning.'

'Only because you—' Claudia stopped. It wouldn't do to let David suspect just how vividly she remembered what had happened. 'I think we agreed that neither of us knew what we were doing,' she said coldly as she wriggled down under the sheet once more. 'If I had realised that it was you, then obviously I wouldn't have touched you.'

David propped himself up on one elbow. 'Why *obviously*?' The dismissive note in her voice had caught him on the raw and he was damned if he was going to let her have the last word after all she had put him through. 'After watching you throw yourself at a man you've never met before, it doesn't seem to me that there's anything obvious about your attitude to men, except perhaps that you're prepared to do absolutely anything to get what you want.'

'There's nothing wrong with knowing what you want,' retorted Claudia, who had often spent anguished evenings wondering just what she wanted from a man. 'At least it helps to know that I *don't* want you!'

'Why?' sneered David. 'Because I don't have the right initials to fulfil some stupid prediction made by someone dressed up in a tent twenty years ago?'

She adjusted her pillow. 'Perhaps it's because I'm only interested in caring, sensitive men,' she said loftily.

'Like Justin Darke?'

'Yes.'

David could see her eyes gleaming defiantly up at him through the darkness. 'I think you're making a big mistake,' he said. 'Justin's not nearly man enough for you.'

'He's more of a man than you are!' she snapped. 'At least he's not afraid to show that he's a real man with real feelings, while you...you've got all the emotional responses of a...a *slug*!'

David had had enough. It had been a long, frustrating day, and throughout it Claudia had been a thorn in his side, irritating, provocative, utterly unignorable. She had twined her arms around his neck and sought his kisses, she had embroiled him in one embarrassing situation after another, she had insulted him in front of Patrick, possibly his most valued member of staff, she had made him drive ten miles when all he wanted to do was sleep and now—*now*!—she dared to lie there and accuse him of having no feelings!

His hand shot out and closed around Claudia's wrist, pulling her across the bed towards him. 'So you think I'm unresponsive, do you, Claudia?' he said through his teeth as he caught her other arm and pinned her beneath him with the weight of his body. 'Did I seem unresponsive this morning?'

'This morning was different,' she said unsteadily, aware too late that she had pushed him too far, and more disturbed than she wanted to admit by the feel of his body against hers.

'How?'

'Well...' She moistened her lips with the tip of her tongue. 'You...you didn't realise that it was me.'

'I know it's you now, though, Claudia, and I don't feel unresponsive at all.' Very slowly, remorselessly, David bent his head.

Claudia braced herself, but instead of capturing her lips as she had expected he touched his mouth to the lobe of her ear and began feathering tiny kisses along her jaw and down the pure line of her throat to where a pulse beat with wild, treacherous response.

She mustn't react, Claudia told herself desperately, but his lips were so warm, so tantalising that she couldn't prevent a prickle of excitement as he stretched out first one arm and then the other. 'Do I feel unresponsive to you?' he murmured remorselessly against her palm before letting his mouth trail from her wrist along the soft skin of her inner arm to her elbow.

'I think you've made your point,' she managed, and tried to tug her arm away.

David released her hand, but his lips were on her shoulder now, exploring the enticing hollow of her clavicle, drifting instinctively to the sensitive skin below her ear. She drew a sharp breath and fought the quiver of response, but David felt it.

'Do I?' he insisted softly against her neck.

'N-no.'

This was ridiculous. She had both hands free now; she could push him away whenever she chose. One part of Claudia's mind urged her to do just that, the other reminded her unfairly that this was what she had been thinking about all day. How could a man with a mouth so stern melt her bones just by touching his lips to her skin? There was something bewitching about his slow, sure kisses. They held her more securely than any grip, and as his mouth found hers at last Claudia succumbed to its invitation with a tiny sigh of release.

Without even being aware of what she was doing, she let her hands slide luxuriously up his shoulders to smooth over the sleek muscles that she remembered so vividly from that morning. David gave a smothered oath and pulled her almost fiercely against him, and the blissfully slow kiss took fire. Its blaze caught them both unawares, both unable to resist the searing excitement that soared so unexpectedly between them.

The tension, the snappy arguments, the provocation…all dissolved in the face of scorching sensation where nothing mattered but the wild urgency of their kisses and the beat of their bodies. David's hands were hard against Claudia's body, and she clung to him, arching with a gasp as he dragged up her T-shirt so that he could take her breast in his mouth while his fingers swept lower to caress the softness of her inner thighs, to slide inside her and discover her flooding warmth.

'David!' Every sense in Claudia's body snarled at his touch, and she cried his name without thinking.

'Claudia,' he whispered in response against her breast, and then, as if he had only just heard what he had said, 'Claudia?'

With an immense effort, he lifted his head. Claudia was lying beneath him, her eyes half closed with desire and her body soft and inviting. Slowly she became aware of his hesitation, and her eyelids lifted languidly. 'David?' she murmured again, before something in his expression filtered through the feelings that swirled around her.

'I don't think either of us can pretend we didn't know what we were doing this time,' said David.

His words hit Claudia like a slap in the face. There was a terrible moment of numb shock before she jerked away from him, trembling with reaction. 'Wh-what did you do that for?' she asked in a voice that sounded nothing like her own.

David pulled out a pillow and shoved it pointedly between them. 'Think of it as a birthday present,' he said, and, turning his back to her, settled himself for sleep.

'I'd like an apology.'

Breakfast had been delivered just as in a hotel, and they had been drinking coffee in silence, cold on Claudia's part, unconcerned on David's. Claudia's initial reaction, after lying awake for hours, her body raging with anger and unsatisfied desire, had been to try and shame David by the dignified way she ignored the whole incident, but so far he hadn't shown any sign of noticing that she was ignoring anything.

Typical, Claudia had fumed. Pretending that nothing had happened might be the easiest option, but it was

probably playing right into David's hands. He was a
man, and in Claudia's experience the last thing any man
wanted was a discussion, especially about emotions, and
especially at breakfast. It wasn't something she particularly wanted to discuss herself, but why should she sit
there and quietly accept the way he had kissed her?
Surely at thirty she was mature enough to talk about sex
without stuttering and stammering and tying herself up
into knots of embarrassment?

So Claudia had put down her cup and demanded an
apology.

'All right, I'm sorry,' said David without looking up
from a paper he was reading.

The casual, almost dismissive apology was not what
Claudia had had in mind at all. She stared across the
table at him with gathering wrath. 'Is that it?'

He glanced up. 'You said you wanted an apology, so
I said I was sorry. What more do you want?'

'Some indication that you knew what you were sorry
for would be a start!'

'I imagine you want me to apologise for kissing you,'
he sighed. 'Personally, I don't see why I should apologise for something we both enjoyed, but if it'll shut you
up I don't mind saying sorry.'

'And that's it, is it?' Claudia was incandescent with
rage. 'You practically rape me and then think that if you
toss a casual "sorry" across the breakfast table I'll shut
up about it!'

David laid the paper he had been reading on the table
with a smack of his hand and faced Claudia, his eyes
cold and grey and very angry. 'Now just a minute!' he
said in a voice that would have cut through steel. 'Are
you going to sit there and try to tell me that you didn't
enjoy it?'

'I didn't want you to kiss me,' Claudia insisted, although she knew it wasn't really an answer to his accusation.

'Then you shouldn't have provoked me,' said David. 'You're not some silly teenager. You're an experienced woman of thirty, and you ought to have known better than to climb into bed beside a man with nothing but a flimsy T-shirt on and start taunting him about not having any reactions!'

'As an *experienced man*,' Claudia flashed back, 'I'm surprised you weren't able to deal with the situation without resorting to brute force!'

They glared at each other across the table for a moment before David capitulated with a shrug. 'OK,' he admitted, 'I'll give you that. I lost my temper and perhaps I shouldn't have kissed you, but you could have pushed me away.'

Claudia's blue-grey eyes were stormy, her cheeks flushed with temper. 'It may not be very gentlemanlike to remind you,' David went on, 'but if it hadn't been for me it would have been a lot more than a kiss, wouldn't it?'

There was a fraught silence. Claudia would have done anything to be able to lie, but she had an innate honesty that dried the outraged denial on her tongue. Her eyes slid away from his. 'Maybe,' she said.

'Maybe?'

'Oh, all right,' she snapped. 'It would.'

'So am I supposed to be apologising for stopping?'

'No!' Claudia glared at David in baffled fury. It wasn't fair, the way he seemed to be able to twist things round so that she ended up not knowing what she felt. 'I thought we agreed a truce?' she muttered sullenly after a moment.

'It doesn't seem to have been a very effective one, does it? Let's agree another. I promise not to kiss you again if you promise not to provoke me.'

'Are we talking about in public or in private?' she said warily.

'I dare say we may have to exchange the odd peck in public, just to look convincing, but that's not really the same thing. There are kisses, and kisses, if you know what I mean.'

The hot colour surged up Claudia's face. 'I know what you mean,' she said tightly.

'So I promise not to touch you when we're alone. Does that seem a fair thing to you?'

For a fleeting moment, Claudia looked into the implacably cool grey eyes and then she looked away. He had an uncanny ability to leave her with nothing to say. 'Yes,' she said.

'So we're agreed?'

'Yes.'

As promised, David dropped her off at Lucy's house before going on to the office to meet up with Patrick and the other senior staff working on the presentation. 'Goodbye, wife,' he said mockingly as he stopped the car. 'Behave. And don't forget the terms of our truce—unless you want me to kiss you again, of course.'

Claudia didn't answer, just slammed the door shut and stalked up the path to the little verandah.

'What was all that about last night?' Lucy pounced on her almost before she was through the door. 'What did you *really* think of him?'

'He's absolutely impossible!' raged Claudia. 'He's smug, arrogant, patronising and utterly hateful!'

'But...I thought you said you liked him?' said Lucy, bewildered.

'I do *not* like him! I hate him!'

Lucy was completely confused. 'Why did you say you thought he was gorgeous, then? Last night you were carrying on as if Justin was the answer to all your prayers.'

'Oh, *Justin*.' Claudia's anger deflated abruptly and her cousin eyed her with a curious expression.

'Who did you think I meant?'

'David,' she admitted, following Lucy into a tiny, functional kitchen and watching her put the kettle on.

'Why, what's he done?'

How could she explain to Lucy about that devastating kiss? Claudia's previous experience of men had left her, if not exactly cynical, at least armoured, and it was a shock to find that the emotions that she'd thought she had so well-ordered could be jumbled up and tossed around by a man she didn't even like!

'It's not what he *does* exactly, it's the way he sits and looks down that long nose of his. He just makes me feel…oh, I don't know…stupid, I suppose.'

'You?' Lucy held out a mug of coffee and looked at her in amazement. Claudia had always been the glamorous, assured one. Lucy couldn't imagine her ever feeling stupid.

Claudia swirled her coffee, staring down at it morosely. 'Is he that unpleasant with everybody or is it just me?'

'I think you must be imagining things,' said Lucy comfortingly. 'I've never seen David anything but charming, and I know him quite well—or as well as anyone out here does. I suppose he can be a bit reserved sometimes, but that's just the way he is. Actually,' she confided, leading the way back to the living room, 'I've always found him very attractive. He's not exactly handsome, but there's something rather sexy about him somehow. His face never gives much away, but he's got a lovely smile, and you get the feeling that behind all that English restraint he's probably incredibly passionate.'

Claudia thought of David's mouth at her breast and a strange sensation shuddered down her spine. 'I can't say

I've noticed,' she said as nonchalantly as she could manage while a voice deep inside her accused her, *Liar!*

'Haven't you?' Lucy sounded surprised. 'I'm sorry you don't like him, though, Claudia, because he's really very nice when you get to know him.' She plumped down on the sofa and put her feet up on the coffee table. 'He's incredibly successful too. The firm was in a mess when he joined, but he's turned everything round and we're bidding for all the prestige projects now. That's why getting this contract for the second phase is so important. A project this size will put the firm right up in the big league, but if the sheikh awards it to someone else it might lead to a loss of confidence. I expect David's a bit preoccupied at the moment and that's why you haven't seen the best side of him.'

'He didn't seem preoccupied when he was talking to you last night,' Claudia was unable to prevent herself pointing out.

If Lucy heard the jealousy in her cousin's voice, she didn't comment on it. 'He's always nice to me,' she admitted. 'A lot of successful people are too full of themselves to waste time on mere wives, but David's always treated us as if we're just as important to him as the engineers.'

Claudia made a show of flicking through the collection of CDs on the shelf. 'Why hasn't he married if he's so nice and successful and generally wonderful?' she asked, keeping her back carefully turned and hoping she sounded as if she couldn't care less one way or the other.

'I don't know,' said Lucy, not without regret. 'I'm sure Patrick does, but he's so boring about never gossiping. I *did* hear that David was engaged once, but I don't know what happened.'

'His fiancée probably couldn't stand being patronised the whole time,' said Claudia sourly to conceal the awful feeling of a stone settling in her stomach at the news that David had loved someone enough to marry her.

Lucy sat up straight and looked at her cousin with renewed interest. 'You really *don't* like him, do you?'

Claudia bit her lip. If Lucy suspected that she was more interested in David than she admitted, she would never let Claudia hear the last of it! She moved casually away from the CDs and sat down on the sofa next to her cousin. 'Why are we wasting time talking about David Stirling?' she said. 'Tell me about Justin instead—he's the one I came here to meet.'

Lucy had known Claudia a long time. Her cousin was behaving very oddly, but if she didn't want Lucy to know what she was up to Lucy wouldn't get anything out of her, so she might as well give up now. If Claudia wanted her to think that she had fallen madly in love with Justin Darke, Lucy would play along with it, but she didn't for one minute believe that it was true.

At lunchtime she bore Claudia off to the 'club', a plain building with a bar, a simple menu and a swimming pool, and they spent the afternoon gossiping happily in the shade. Claudia was relieved that Lucy seemed to have accepted her supposed attraction to Justin so readily. After last night's kiss, it was more important than ever that David thought her interest was firmly fixed on another, and she didn't want Lucy telling him that she was behaving completely out of character. She had enough to cope with trying not to think about David, about the feel of his lips and the touch of his hands and the fact that she was going to have to get back into bed beside him again that night.

One thing was for certain—she wasn't going to let David know that she was bothered by the prospect. 'You're not a silly teenager,' he had said, and it was time she stopped behaving like one. Claudia wasn't at all sure that she liked the implications of being catego-

rised as an experienced woman, but if experienced
women were cool and composed and capable of dealing
with potentially embarrassing situations with poise, then
that was what she would be. From now on, David would
have no excuse to deliver the kind of stinging comments
he had that morning.

He sent a car to pick her up from Lucy's later that
afternoon, and was sorting out papers in the guest quarters when she came in. He looked up but carried on
working, and Claudia found herself gripped by an unexpected shyness. 'How did your meeting go?' she
asked, standing awkwardly by the door.

'Very well. We've still a long way to go, though.' He
laid a plan on a pile and straightened from the table,
looking at Claudia as if for the first time. She was wearing cool linen trousers and a plain white top, and her
skin was flushed with the heat. The silky blonde hair
was pushed behind her ears, and she had a curiously
vulnerable air as she stood just inside the room as if
uncertain of her welcome. He looked away. 'How was
your day?'

'Fine.'

An uncomfortable silence fell. Really, it was easier
when they were fighting, thought Claudia almost desperately. There never seemed to be any problem thinking
of what to say then!

'I gather we're ordered back to Lucy's for some
party,' said David at last. 'What time are we expected?'

'About half past seven.'

David flexed his shoulders as if they were stiff. He
looked tired, Claudia realised. Perhaps he hadn't slept as
much last night as she had thought. 'You don't need to
come if you don't want to,' she said impulsively. 'I'm
sure Lucy wouldn't mind if you stayed here.'

'I'm sure she wouldn't,' he agreed sardonically. 'But

if you'd planned to spend the evening chatting up Justin without me I'm afraid I'm going to disappoint you both.'

Claudia opened her mouth to deny any such intention, and then shut it again. What was the point?

'Besides,' David went on, 'news of our wedding has got round with phenomenal speed. Lucy's billed this as your birthday party, but everyone is obviously going to treat it as a celebration of our supposed marriage, so I can hardly stay at home, can I?'

Obscurely hurt by the resumption of his suspicious manner, Claudia took immense pains getting ready for the party, and when she had finished she knew she looked her best. She wore a stunning cream dress that stopped above the knee, and the gold shoes made her legs look even longer and even slimmer. The dress was so simple that she could get away with wittily excessive jewellery, so she had on an oversized chunky gold necklace and matching earrings that were agony on her earlobes but worth the effort for their effect.

Would David think she looked good? He might think the jewellery was a bit over-the-top, but surely even he couldn't complain about the dress.

David was caught unawares when she emerged from the bathroom, and for a moment he could only stare and struggle for breath. 'All this effort for Justin?' he mocked when he thought he could speak without gasping. 'Are you sure he's worth it?'

Claudia struggled with her disappointment at his lack of reaction. Well, what had she been expecting? That he would sweep her up into his arms and tell her that she looked beautiful? Fool, she told herself ferociously. What do you care what he thinks, anyway?

'I don't know,' she said evenly after a moment. 'But I'm going to enjoy finding out.'

David's face darkened. 'Can I remind you that these are all my employees you're going to meet this eve-

ning?' he said with a snap. 'I'd rather you didn't spend
the whole time hanging on Justin's every word. Try and
act like a girl I might conceivably marry, if that's not
too difficult for you.'

'And what sort of girl is that?' asked Claudia sweetly.
'Just so I know what to pretend, of course.'

'I'd only want to marry a girl who was honest, unaffected and sensible,' said David. 'And they're not
qualities that I've seen much in evidence in you so far,
so I just hope you're a good actress!'

CHAPTER SEVEN

LUCY'S house seemed to be full of people when they arrived, and the sound of voices and laughter spilled out into the still desert night. David and Claudia hesitated by the car in the darkness. 'Do you really think everyone is going to believe that we're married?' Claudia whispered, suddenly unsure of herself.

'Why shouldn't they? The main thing is that nobody would expect us to be lying, so as long as you can keep your hands off Justin Darke they're not likely to suspect that we're not exactly what we say we are. All we have to do is look suitably in love,' David added with an ironic edge to his voice that brought a flush to her cheeks.

'I'm not sure I know how to look as if I'm in love with you,' she snapped.

'Just look like you did when you were kissing me last night,' said David unfairly. 'That ought to do the trick.'

Distinctly ruffled, Claudia bit back an extremely unladylike answer and would have stalked up to the door in high dudgeon if David hadn't caught hold of her arm. 'If you go in looking like that, they'll all think we're well on our way to being divorced already,' he muttered.

'It can't come soon enough for me!' retorted Claudia.

'You're breaking my heart,' said David, deadpan, and took her hand in a firm grip. 'Now we're going to go in, and smile and pretend we're madly in love with each other, and we're going to remember our truce, aren't we?'

His voice held an undercurrent of steel, and although

110

Claudia's eyes were still mutinous somehow she found herself saying, 'Yes.'

She was very conscious of his strong fingers around hers as they walked up the path and into the house. There was a good-natured cheer when they appeared, and then Lucy swooped on them with a shriek. 'Claudia, you look so grown-up!' she cried, hugging her cousin.

'That's because I'm thirty and you've still got five months to go,' said Claudia. 'When you're as old as I am, you'll look grown-up too. As soon as you hit the big three-oh, you're supposed to miraculously become glamorous and assured and at ease with your own body.'

'Well, it seems to have worked for you,' said Lucy admiringly. She turned to give David a warm hug of welcome. 'Doesn't she look beautiful?'

David watched Patrick lift Claudia off the ground in a bear hug and was caught off guard by a stab of something that might almost have been jealousy at the sight of another man's arms around that slender body. She was laughing, her eyes alight and very blue tonight, and her face vivid with warmth. Had he really only thought her 'pretty enough' when he first saw her? She was more than pretty tonight. She looked vibrant and alive and, yes, beautiful.

'Yes,' he said in an odd voice.

'Everybody knows about your secret marriage,' Lucy was telling him in an undertone. 'So I'm afraid you might be in for a toast and a few speeches.'

He groaned, although he was glad at the change of subject. 'Didn't you tell them we didn't want any fuss?'

'Of course, but you can't stop people being pleased for you.' She smiled at him. 'They're fond of you, David. Just think of it as a practice run for when you do the real thing!'

David tried to imagine being married, walking into a room like this with another woman at his side, but when he tried to picture her Claudia's image kept getting in the way and he frowned. If he ever took the plunge, it wouldn't be with anyone like her.

Claudia was still chatting comfortably with Patrick. She never looked that relaxed and happy with *him*, David realised, and for some reason the thought left him feeling vaguely disgruntled. 'I think once will be quite enough,' he said to Lucy, and went over to take Claudia's hand. She was supposed to belong to him this evening, after all.

His fingers closing around hers sent a dangerous thrill down Claudia's spine and quite involuntarily she returned the clasp of his hand. His strength seemed to flow into her, insensibly reassuring, but when she glanced up at him his face was quite unreadable. He had changed into a clean white short-sleeved shirt with pale trousers, and managed in that simple outfit to look cool and restrained but somehow tough at the same time.

'Come on,' he said. 'We'd better circulate.'

As Lucy had warned, everyone was eager to meet Claudia and offer warm congratulations on their marriage. No one seemed to find it in the least odd that they had apparently married on such a short acquaintance.

'What's the point in waiting?' said a comfortable-looking woman in her fifties. 'You're both old enough to know your own minds, so why should you hang around?'

'I never wanted a big wedding,' Claudia offered, feeling that she should make some contribution to the conversation. 'I always felt that what matters is the commitment that the two people concerned make to each other, not the size of the cake or the colour of the tablecloths.'

'Quite right,' the woman agreed roundly. 'All that matters is that you and David love each other—and it's easy to see that you do *that*!'

'Is it?' David managed a polite smile. 'We thought we'd hidden it rather well.'

'Oh, no, it's obvious when two people are in love. They get a sort of glow about them—I could see it as soon as you and Claudia walked into the room.'

Claudia didn't dare look at David. 'Really?' she said weakly, but when someone else asked how they had met her mind went completely blank. Had they agreed on a story? 'You tell them, darling,' she said, throwing all the responsibility onto David.

If David was thrown, he didn't show it. 'We were sitting next to each other on a plane,' he said, wondering what they would say if they knew that the plane in question had taken off less than forty-eight hours ago.

'Oh, how romantic! Was it love at first sight?'

David didn't answer immediately. He reached out and smoothed a pale gold strand very carefully behind Claudia's ear. 'Not quite,' he said softly. 'But it didn't take long, did it, Claudia?'

Claudia had the oddest impression that the floor had dropped away beneath her feet, leaving her dangling over an abyss of dark and dangerous desire. David's fingers had been gentle as they'd brushed against her cheek, but she could feel her skin tingling where he had touched her. She thought about her first sight of him, sitting so cool and self-contained in the hubbub of the departure lounge. She thought about the hard strength of his body and strange sense of security she had when she was with him. She thought about his mouth and his hands and the way he looked when he couldn't decide whether to be angry or amused, and she felt suddenly jarred and breathless. She didn't want to look down into the abyss and see what was there.

They were all waiting for her to say something, smiling expectantly. Claudia gulped at her champagne. 'No, not long,' she croaked.

It was almost a relief when they were swept up into different groups and he wasn't standing so distractingly close, but in another way it was worse. People kept asking her about the wedding, about the honeymoon, what David had given her for her birthday, and all the time Claudia was aware of him on the other side of the room.

She answered vaguely, awarding herself a future honeymoon in the Seychelles and a sapphire and diamond ring for her birthday as the first things that came into her head, but her mind was on David, standing so cool and contained, talking to others, smiling at others. He smiled at everyone except her.

It was impossible not to notice how he dominated the room. He wasn't taller or louder or more flamboyant than anyone else—quite the opposite—but there was a compelling quality about him, a power and a presence that somehow made him the focus of everything.

He wasn't yet forty, Claudia remembered, but he had the authority of a much older man, especially compared to the other men in the room, most of whom, apart from the senior engineers, were still in their twenties and at the start of their careers. With something of a shock, Claudia realised that she no longer identified automatically with them. She was thirty now, and somehow it seemed to put her in a different category, and for the first time it struck her that she didn't even want to be twenty again. A wry smile touched her lips. Perhaps she had grown up overnight after all?

'I've been trying to meet you all evening.' A young engineer who introduced himself as Pete broke into her thoughts as he dragged her aside and studied her with frank interest. 'You're not at all what I imagined you to be like when I heard David had married.'

He had such a disarming smile that Claudia couldn't help smiling back at him. 'Why, what were you expecting?'

'I thought you'd be like his other girlfriends,' said Pete. 'But, having seen you, I'm not at all surprised that he decided to marry someone quite different. You look like much more fun!'

Other girlfriends? *What* other girlfriends? Claudia's eyes narrowed. 'Oh? I didn't realise I wasn't running true to type! What were his other girlfriends like?'

Belatedly, Pete realised that he had blundered onto dangerous ground. 'Oh, well, I didn't really know any of them very well. I only saw them when he took them to the firm's ball or functions like that when I was based in London. They were all very nice,' he said, not at all sure about Claudia's expression. 'Very pretty, very sweet...but David didn't look at them the way he looks at you.'

Claudia could believe it. David wouldn't look at sweet, pretty, *nice* girls with irritation or dislike or contempt, the way he looked at her. Realising that her fingers were curled into fists and that her nails were digging into her palms, she flexed them surreptitiously. She didn't want Pete to think that she was jealous, did she? What did it matter to *her* if David had a whole harem of sweet, pretty girls waiting nicely for him in London?

'Who's that he's talking to now?' she asked lightly. David was standing near the door, laughing with Justin Darke and a petite, pretty girl of about twenty.

Pete was patently relieved at the change of subject. 'Oh, that's Justin Darke. He's an American architect.'

'I've met Justin. I meant the girl.'

Pete's view was blocked by David's back, but he craned his neck to see. 'That's John Phillips's daughter, Fiona. She's a student, I think, just out to visit her parents during the university vacation. Nice girl,' he added.

Claudia's eyes narrowed. It was obvious from the way that David was smiling down at Fiona that he thought she was nice, too. She was certainly pretty, and no doubt she was sweet as well. And she was *young*. Looking at that fresh young skin and innocent expression, Claudia forgot about how she had just convinced herself that she was happy being thirty. Who wanted to be mature and thirty when you could have the bloom of twenty? she thought gloomily.

And who wanted to be glamorous and assured when you could be honest and unaffected and sensible, and all those other things that made up David's ideal woman? Fiona seemed to have everything going for her...but then it wasn't Fiona that David was supposed to be married to this evening, Claudia remembered. It might be as well to remind David of that fact as well!

Murmuring an excuse, she left Pete and headed over towards David. It was obviously high time he was reminded of her existence! 'Hello,' she said with a brittle smile as she came up to him. Her chin was up, her eyes bright with challenge, and she tucked her hand very deliberately into David's arm. 'I've been missing you.'

David eyed her warily, wondering what had happened to put the glitter back in her eyes. He hoped she'd been behaving herself. Whenever he'd looked over at her during the evening, she had seemed to be on sparkling form, but God only knew what she had been saying. He'd had some very strange comments about their honeymoon plans. At least she hadn't monopolised Justin all evening. In fact, David admitted grudgingly to himself, this was the first time she had come near the American all evening. Nobody would ever guess that he was the only reason she was here at all.

'Claudia, this is Fiona Phillips.' He wished he weren't so aware of her standing so close to him. He could feel her fingers against his bare arm, and smell her perfume. 'And you know Justin, of course,' he finished woodenly.

'Of course. It's lovely to see you again so soon.' David wasn't surprised to see the warm smile Claudia bestowed on Justin, but he was taken aback when she slid her hand down his arm and twined her fingers with his, leaning artlessly against him as she said hello to Fiona. What was she playing at?

'Justin said you were in television.' Fiona had big brown eyes, soft curls and a sweet expression, her face fresh and pretty and free of make-up.

'That's right,' said Claudia grandly. 'I work for a production company.'

'I would love to get into something like that when I graduate,' sighed Fiona. 'It sounds so exciting!'

'Well, it can be a bit hectic...' In spite of herself, Claudia was disarmed by the girl's evident admiration. David's arm was tense against hers, his fingers stiff. His face was expressionless but Claudia knew perfectly well that he was irritated. Television was obviously much too glamorous for David to deal with. All those nice girl-friends of his probably had caring, meaningful jobs where everyone wore sensible clothes and problems were discussed in a calm, understanding way.

Well, let him realise just how different a girl he was dealing with now! Deliberately, Claudia began to show off, making Fiona and Justin laugh with stories of disastrous productions she had been involved with while David's smile grew increasingly forced.

'You're not going to give up your job, are you?' said Fiona, wiping her eyes after Claudia had finished telling them about a mini-series that had been distinguished by more drama off the set than on.

'Give up my job?' Claudia echoed, astonished. 'Of course not! It's taken me long enough to get this far!'

'I meant because of your marriage,' the other girl explained.

'Oh.' Claudia had been so carried away with her story-telling that she had almost forgotten what she was doing there. 'Well, I certainly don't plan on leaving work yet. I'd go mad sitting around all day waiting for David to come home.' She glanced at David's rigid jaw. 'Of course,' she added provocatively, 'it'll be different when we have a family.'

'You're planning to have children, then?'

'Definitely,' said Claudia, peeping another glance from under her lashes to see the muscle beating in David's clenched jaw.

Fiona was looking dewy-eyed. 'How many?'

'Well, I'd like six, but David thinks four would be enough.' She rubbed her cheek winsomely against his shoulder. There was no harm in making sure that everyone knew just who he was supposed to be married to. 'Don't you, darling?'

'Quite enough,' said David, with a warning glance that Claudia met with wide, innocent eyes. Six children, ye Gods! Were they supposed to be part of Justin's destiny too?

'Can I have your attention for a moment, please?' Patrick was banging a knife against his glass, and the room fell obediently silent as they all turned to face him. David's heart sank. God, how had he ever let himself get into this situation?

'I've been asked to say a few words to welcome Claudia and David here tonight,' Patrick went on a little desperately, meeting David's eyes with mute apology. He looked almost as uncomfortable as David felt. 'I'm not a great hand at speeches, so I won't prolong the agony, but we all want to congratulate you on your marriage, and wish you both much happiness together.'

'And we forgive you for not asking us to the wedding,' someone at the back shouted, to much laughter.

Suddenly Claudia became aware that a space had cleared around her and David, leaving them isolated and on show in the middle of the floor. David released her hand to put an arm around her waist instead as they stood as if at bay, surrounded by smiling, expectant stares.

'Speech!' they called.

Claudia mentally thanked her lucky stars that the bride was never called upon to make a speech. David had no such comfort. 'Thank you all very much,' he said, and she couldn't help but be impressed by his composure. He looked as cool and relaxed as ever, and only the tension in the hand at her waist betrayed his discomfort. 'I wish we could have invited all of you to the wedding, but to tell the truth it was just as much of a surprise to us to find ourselves married as it is to you!'

They all laughed. They thought he was joking.

'Visiting a construction site in the middle of the desert isn't an ideal start to married life, but I think it's given Claudia some idea of what she's let herself in for, and we're both very grateful to you for making her so welcome.' David hesitated, glancing down at the blonde head at his shoulder. 'It's been a big week for Claudia. Not only did she find herself married, but she turned thirty yesterday. I'm not sure if either of those experiences was quite what she expected, but she's coped with both in her own inimitable style, so perhaps you would all join me in a toast—to Claudia!'

Lifting his glass to her, David smiled almost ruefully as Claudia lifted blue, puzzled eyes to meet his. She looked stunned, and he didn't blame her. The words had just come out, and they had taken him aback as much as her.

'To Claudia!' rippled round the room as glasses were raised, but she heard them only vaguely. Her heart was booming in her ears, and she smiled uncertainly, knowing that something was expected of her but unable to tear her gaze from his. His eyes were light, arrested, mesmerising, and when his arm tightened around her she lifted her face instinctively.

David, too, felt strangely detached. He hadn't intended to pull Claudia closer any more than he had intended to toast her, but his body didn't seem to be following instructions from his brain, and when she turned her face up to his it seemed obvious to gather Claudia closer and touch his mouth to hers.

Even as he bent his head, David told himself that it would be a brief, impersonal kiss to satisfy all those watching with sentimental eyes, but somehow it didn't work out that way. Her lips were warm and enticing, and they parted beneath his as if it were the most natural thing in the world for him to be kissing her, and then, without either of them being aware of quite how it had happened, the kiss took on a life of its own, drawing them in, tangling them up in honeyed sweetness, bewitching them with its promise.

Claudia felt herself spinning slowly, deliciously. Unthinkingly, one arm crept round his back, and her other hand lifted to clutch at his shirt-front for support as she melted against him. Lucy, Patrick, the watching crowd, all had evaporated, leaving her alone with David, and quite deliberately she closed her mind to what had gone before. She didn't want to think about what David had said and what he had done; she wanted only to cling to his strength, to feel his arm hard around her, to taste his mouth and know that for these few moments at least he was hers.

'Aaaahh!' Someone watching heaved a sentimental sigh. It penetrated David's consciousness and, belatedly aware of his loss of control, he tried to lift his head. He even managed to break the kiss, but before he could draw breath his mouth had sought Claudia's once more, and they were drifting blissfully again.

With an enormous effort of will, David forced himself to let her go. He felt jolted, jarred, completely disorien-

tated, and when the crowd erupted into cheers and whis-
tles he had to shake his head slightly to readjust.

Claudia hardly even heard the applause. Her legs felt
as if they were about to buckle beneath her, and she had
to cling onto David for support while the last wisps of
enchantment cleared and left her burning with self-
consciousness. Had that really been her, melting into
David's arms as if that was all she had been thinking
about all evening?

To complete her discomfiture, Lucy was heading towards them, grinning from ear to ear. 'That was brilliant,' she congratulated them out of the corner of her
mouth. 'No one would ever suspect you weren't besotted
with each other!' She winked at Claudia. 'You're wasted
behind the camera, coz. After that performance, I think
you should take up acting!'

Performance. Acting. Lucy's words were as effective
as a dash of icy water in bringing them down to earth.
David and Claudia jerked away from each other and then
stood feeling ridiculously awkward. David was still
holding a glass in one hand and he looked down at it as
if wondering how it had got there.

Claudia's lips were throbbing, her blood pounding,
and she didn't know what to do with her hands. They
had felt so right holding onto David, but now they just
dangled uselessly, emptily, and when someone offered
her another glass of champagne she grabbed at it and
drank half of it in one gulp in an attempt to steady her
shaken nerves.

'I'm sorry about that, David,' Patrick muttered, join-
ing them. 'I tried to persuade them that you didn't want
any fuss, but they insisted that I made a speech.'

'Don't worry about it.' David cleared his throat and
pulled himself together with an effort.

'Weren't they convincing, though?' said Lucy.

Patrick looked from David to Claudia. They both

looked as if they were reeling with reaction and only grasping reality with difficulty. 'Very convincing,' he said dryly.

Claudia couldn't look at David. He seemed to be able to carry on a perfectly normal conversation with Patrick while she was left feeling horribly exposed and fighting the terrible urge to hide herself back in the shelter of David's arm. Petrified that she would do just that, she edged away, and it was almost a relief when she was swept up into another group and out of temptation.

The evening became a blur of smiling faces. It seemed that everyone wanted to tell her how right she and David looked together. Claudia nodded and smiled and did her best to say the right thing, but it was impossible to concentrate. Couldn't everyone see that she was still glowing after David's kiss? Couldn't they tell how the nerves were fluttering under her skin and churning in her stomach? She didn't know whether she longed for this evening to end, or dreaded the time when she and David were alone. How could she pretend to be cool and aloof when her body was still quivering from his kiss?

Overwhelmed by the feeling that everything was spinning out of her control, Claudia slipped out onto the verandah. Justin was sitting alone on one of the chairs, and he got to his feet with a smile when he saw her. 'You look like you could do with a break,' he said. 'Is it all getting a bit much in there?'

'Something like that,' she admitted. She sank down into a chair and closed her eyes, enjoying the feel of the cool night air against her flushed skin. They sat in companionable silence for a moment, then Claudia opened her eyes. 'What are you doing out here?'

'I guess it all got a bit much for me, too,' he said with a brief smile. 'I wanted to think.'

'I'm sorry, I shouldn't have interrupted you,' she began, but Justin waved a denial.

'No, I'm glad you're here. To tell you the truth, I was just thinking about you and David. It's so great to see you two together.' He paused, looked out into the night. 'My parents split up when I was a kid, and I always swore I'd never let myself in for that kind of mess, but somehow, when you meet someone special, you begin to think that maybe it's worth taking the risk after all.' He glanced at Claudia with a half-smile. 'You and David obviously decided to take the risk.'

'We haven't been married very long,' she said, uncomfortably aware that she might be inviting confidences she did not deserve.

Justin shook his head. 'There's a real bond between you, anyone can see that. You don't hang around each other like some couples do, but even when you're on opposite sides of the room it's obvious that you're aware of each other. It's a sort of electricity, I guess,' he said. 'I noticed it as soon as I met you.'

'Really?' said Claudia faintly.

'Sure.' Justin hesitated again. 'Do you think marriage is safer the older you get?' he asked in a rush at last, and then grimaced as he heard what he had said. 'I'm sorry, that sounded rude! I didn't mean it.'

Claudia couldn't help laughing at his dismay. 'It's all right,' she said. 'Thirty's not exactly ancient, but I know what you mean. The older you are, the more chance you've had to look around and decide what you really want out of a relationship.'

'Exactly,' said Justin, grateful for her understanding. 'That makes it less of a risk, doesn't it? Less than if you were marrying someone much younger...say, about twenty?'

His tone was elaborately casual, but Claudia wasn't fooled. It sounded as if Justin had someone very definite in mind. It was just as well she hadn't really been banking on him as her destiny, she thought with some amusement.

'Well,' she said carefully, 'I don't think there's ever an ideal age to get married. You could say that there's always a risk involved. You never know just how things are going to work out, but as long as you feel that the person you're marrying is the one you want to spend the rest of your life with, then I don't think it matters whether they're twenty or forty or sixty.'

'There's ten years between you and David, isn't there?' said Justin, still pursuing his own line of thought. 'Do you think it would have been the same for you and David if you'd met ten years ago, when you were twenty and he was thirty?'

Claudia thought of herself at twenty. There hadn't been any lines around her eyes then and her skin had had the bloom of a peach, but she had been awkward and insecure, trying to disguise her lack of confidence behind a bravado that had probably come across as arrogance, and just as probably would have fooled no one. Somehow she didn't think David would have liked her any better then than he did now. She smiled rather sadly. 'It's hard to know but I think we would have felt just the same about each other.'

Justin drew a deep breath as if a great weight had been lifted off his shoulders. 'I'm so glad I talked to you, Claudia. You've been wonderful—' He broke off and looked up as a figure appeared in the door. 'Oh, hi, David!'

Claudia swung round in her chair to see David, tall and solid and overwhelmingly distinct in the doorway. The light was behind him, and it was impossible to read his expression, but his sudden appearance was enough to drive all the air from her lungs. For a fraction of a second, she felt suspended, oddly empty, and then breath and sensation came back with a great whoosh that swept right through her and left her tingling with an electric awareness from fingertips to toes. She couldn't have spoken if she had tried.

Justin was getting to his feet. 'Were you looking for your wife?' he asked good-humouredly.

'I was,' said David. To Claudia, his voice sounded detached, indifferent, and she looked at him uncertainly. 'But she seems to be quite happy where she is.'

'She's a great lady,' Justin told him warmly. 'She's been giving me some good advice about marriage.'

'Has she, now?' David's smile didn't reach his eyes. He was shaken to discover how much he hated the idea of Claudia sitting out here with the American, giving him advice in the darkness, being a *great lady*.

He forced himself to relax his hands, which had bunched quite instinctively into fists, and concentrated on breathing normally. 'It's getting late. I wondered if you were ready to go?' he said to Claudia, carefully polite.

'Yes.' Constrained by a sudden strait-jacket of shyness, oddly hurt by the remoteness in his expression which suggested that he hadn't cared at all that she was sitting out in the dark with Justin, Claudia stood up as well. 'Yes, I'm ready.'

She didn't look at David as they said their goodbyes to Lucy and Patrick. It seemed to take an agonisingly long time to get outside again. They had to keep stopping for more farewells, and endless suggestive comments about how eager they were to leave the party early so that they could be on their own, and all the time David rested his hand lightly, politely against Claudia's spine where it sent shivers of awareness rippling through her.

At last, they made it to the door and out into the welcome darkness. David dropped his hand as soon as there was no one to watch them, and they walked without speaking to the car. The music spilling out from the house just seemed to emphasise the silence between them as they got into the car.

When he clicked on the headlights, the glow lit up David's profile. Claudia could see the forceful line of his nose and chin, and she had a sudden, startlingly physical sense of him as a man. Not David, successful engineer and employer; not David, irritable and infuriating companion of the last three days; but David as flesh and blood, David with a beating heart and skin that was warm and exciting against hers.

Claudia felt the air leak out of her lungs as she looked, and a deep, disquieting desire uncurled inside her. What would it be like if they were really married, if they really did want to be on their own? What if they were driving through the night, like now, but knowing that as soon as the door of the guest house closed behind them David would turn and smile and pull her into his arms?

Wrenching her eyes away from him, Claudia drew an unsteady breath. What was the matter with her this evening? They weren't married, and they didn't want to be alone, and judging by the cool indifference on David's face when he had found her with Justin he had no intention of making love to her when they got back.

Not that she wanted him to, Claudia reminded herself hurriedly. She had just been…wondering…that was all.

The noise of the engine was a good excuse for not talking in the car, but when David drew up outside the guest quarters and switched off the engine the silence settled oppressively around them. As David let her into the room and turned to close the door behind them, Claudia felt oddly disorientated, as if that silly little fantasy in the car was about to become real.

All he had to do now was turn back to look at her where she was standing awkwardly in the middle of the room. He wouldn't even need to smile. All he had to do was say 'come here' very softly, and she would be able to go over and lean against him with a sigh. His arms would close around her and she could lift her face to his and then, *then*, he might smile...

CHAPTER EIGHT

WHEN David turned, she even caught her breath as if in anticipation, but he didn't look at her. He didn't hold out his arms and he didn't smile. He just tossed the keys onto a sideboard and then stood, like Claudia, as if unsure what to do next. The only sound was the faint whirring of the air-conditioning.

'I think it went all right, don't you?' said Claudia, unable to bear it any longer. Her voice sounded thin and high, but it was better than that awful, tight silence.

'Yes,' said David.

She took off her earrings with trembling fingers. 'No one seemed to suspect that we weren't married, anyway,' she tried again.

'No,' he said.

Claudia turned the earrings awkwardly in her hands. 'Everyone was very nice, weren't they?' she persevered.

'Yes,' he said.

There was another agonising pause and then David strode over to open the sliding door that led out to the courtyard as if he needed air. He stood in the doorway, his hands thrust into the pockets of his trousers. 'I'm sorry about that kiss,' he said as if the words had been forced out of him.

That kiss. The memory of the piercing sweetness that had caught them both unawares seemed to shimmer in the air between them.

Claudia moistened her lips. 'Th-that's all right,' she said unevenly after a moment.

Another silence. 'I meant what I said about not kissing you,' David went on abruptly at last. 'I'd hoped it wouldn't be necessary but...' He trailed off. It hadn't been necessary at all. A brief peck on the cheek, even a squeeze of her shoulders would have been enough, but how could he explain to Claudia how her perfume had gone to his head? He had found her within the circle of his arm and her face had been tilted up to his and her eyes had been deep and beguiling, and kissing her had seemed to be the most natural thing in the world.

'It doesn't matter,' said Claudia with difficulty. 'I could see that everyone was expecting you to kiss me.'

'Yes.' He ought to be glad that she had assumed that it was part of the performance, David thought heavily. Had she just been playing her part, or had she too felt the kiss slipping out of control? 'I just didn't want you to think that I'd forgotten our agreement,' he ploughed on, even as he wondered why he had started this. 'I said that if I had to kiss you in public it would be no more than a peck, and I suppose it was a bit more than that this evening—'

Claudia's cheeks were scarlet with embarrassment. Was he trying to tell her that he blamed her for letting the kiss get out of control? 'Really, it doesn't matter,' she interrupted him desperately.

David turned to face her at last. 'It won't happen again, in public or private,' he promised.

'Fine,' she said thinly, wondering why she felt like crying.

David eyed Claudia uneasily. She looked upset, her cheeks flushed and her eyes suspiciously bright. He wished he'd never started this excruciating conversation, but he was very conscious that she had kept her part of the bargain. It had never occurred to anybody to doubt that she was his wife, and she had played the role with aplomb. By the end of the evening he'd been sick of being told how wonderful she was, and how right the two of them seemed together, but David was well aware that if she had refused to carry on pretending to be his wife there would have been little he could have done about it, and he felt as if he owed it to her to reassure her that he hadn't intended to take advantage of her.

Claudia was fiddling edgily with her earrings. The air between them twanged with tension and David moved abruptly away from the door, desperate as she had been earlier to break the ghastly silence. 'You and Justin seemed to be getting on well.' The words almost choked him, but it was the only way he could think of to show her that the kiss hadn't meant anything.

'Yes,' she said dispiritedly.

'You were out there together for a long time.' David wanted to sound casual, disinterested, but was appalled to hear the jealous edge to his voice.

Claudia heard accusation, not jealousy. 'I didn't know he was out there,' she explained quickly. 'I just wanted some air—I was tired of lying. Justin was sitting on the verandah, and I could hardly turn round and go in as soon as I'd seen him.' God, why was she excusing herself to *David*?

David hunched his shoulders. 'He seemed very impressed with you.'

'That's not what you said last night.' Her eyes followed him accusingly as he prowled around the room.

'It was different last night,' he said, and then stopped. '*I* feel different,' he admitted honestly.

Claudia's heart began to pound. 'Oh?' she said weakly.

'We were both tired last night, and we seemed to have got ourselves into an unnecessarily complicated situation.' David turned on his heel, dug his hands deeper into his pockets. 'I think what I'm trying to say is that I appreciate what you've been doing. It can't be easy to pretend to be married to a perfectly strange man, but you've done a pretty good job, and I'm sure that only

Patrick and Lucy have any idea that we're not what we say we are.'

He hesitated. 'You've kept your part of the agreement, so it's only fair that I keep mine. You came here to meet Justin Darke, and you should have a chance to do that.' He drew a deep breath, forced himself on. 'It's none of my business how you pursue that relationship, as long as it doesn't make anyone question our supposed marriage for the next two weeks.

'I'm sorry if I've been a little brusque,' he went on, determined to make a clean breast of it. 'I'm very concerned about getting this new contract, and I'm afraid I've taken it out on you, but it seems to me that we're two mature adults, and it ought to be possible for us both to get what we want, so from now on I promise not to interfere with you and Justin.'

It wasn't, somehow, what Claudia had wanted to hear. 'Thank you,' she said dully. 'I'm sure everything will work out for both of us.'

David had been honest, frank, matter-of-fact. What more could she want? Now they both knew where they stood. The conversation should have cleared the air, but if anything the tension between them was even worse as they got ready for bed. There was no need to put a pillow between them that night, Claudia reflected dully. The jangling atmosphere was a more effective barrier than a six-foot wall with broken glass on top.

Claudia lay on her side and stared stoically at the wall, while every nerve in her back quivered with the knowledge that David was lying only inches away. Last night she had lain awake, shaken and angry after the callous way he had kissed her, but tonight...tonight it was different. There hadn't been anything callous about the kiss they had shared tonight. It had been intoxicatingly sweet, ensnaring them both in delight, and she hadn't wanted it to end.

And now they were lying together in the darkness. If she rolled over, and he rolled over, they would be in each other's arms. She could run her hand over his flank and burrow into his strength, and they could let the delight sweep them on and up together into joy.

Only David had made it clear that he didn't want that. 'It won't happen again...' he had said. As long as nothing threatened his reputation with the sheikh, she could spend her holiday as she had planned, doing whatever she pleased with whoever she pleased. That was what she wanted...wasn't it?

The first thing that David saw when he awoke early the next morning was Claudia's face only inches from his. Some time during the night she had turned towards him, and she was lying on her side, one hand curled by her cheek, her other arm flung across the sheet between them so that her fingertips were almost grazing his side. She was sound asleep, her breathing deep and slow, and without those expressive smoky eyes distracting him David was able to study her as if he had never seen her properly before.

Her skin was soft and smooth and faintly flushed with sleep, and the pale gold hair tumbled over her face. Her lips were curved in a slight smile as she dreamt, and something about the way the long dark lashes swept against her cheek wrenched at David's heart. He tried to remind himself of how intensely irritating she could be. She was vain and selfish and thoroughly spoilt. Yes, she was pretty—all right, she was beautiful—but he had fallen in love with a beautiful face before, and there was no way he was going through all that again.

He certainly wasn't about to make a fool of himself over Claudia Cook, who was only interested in fulfilling some ridiculous prediction with Justin Darke.

Claudia sighed and stirred in her sleep, rolling onto

her back and flinging her arm above her head in an unconsciously sensuous gesture. The movement twisted the
T-shirt, stretching it over her breasts, and David drew a
sharp breath and forced himself out of bed. Standing
under the shower, he turned the tap to cold. He was *not*
going to make a fool of himself over her.

Absolutely, definitely not.

Claudia woke to find that David had gone. She told herself that she was glad, but the room seemed curiously
empty without him, and when the phone rang while she
was having breakfast she was furious with herself for
being disappointed when it was only Lucy.

'I'll ring the office and get them to send a driver for
you,' said Lucy, who was unsurprised to hear that David
had already left. 'Patrick was off at the crack of dawn
as well,' she said. 'They're going to be tied up all morning, but he said he would try and meet us for lunch at
the club.'

Lucy was already sitting by the pool by the time
Claudia arrived. 'Well, if it isn't Mrs Stirling!' she
grinned. 'I can't tell you how many times people said to
me what a lovely couple you and David made last
night—it was all I could do to keep a straight face!'

Claudia's answering smile was rather forced. 'It's
amazing how easy it is to make people believe what you
tell them, isn't it?'

'I'll say. If I hadn't known better, I would have believed that you and David were madly in love myself.'
Lucy eyed her cousin speculatively. 'You were really
very convincing, you know. I thought you didn't like
David?'

'Oh, well...' Claudia shrugged, aware that she needed
to tread very carefully. If she insisted that she hated him,
Lucy would just get suspicious. On the other hand, she
didn't want Lucy to think that she *did* like him. She

didn't want anyone to think that, not even herself. 'That was just because I was in a bad mood,' she said as casually as she could. 'I don't *dis*like him. I just wish I didn't have to spend so much time with him when I'd much rather get to know Justin better.'

'I thought you'd like Justin,' said Lucy, apparently accepting Claudia's explanation. 'He's a star, isn't he? He thinks you're wonderful, too. I gather you had quite a chat with him last night. After you'd left, he kept going on about how great you were.' She sighed. 'It's a pity he has to think that you're married to his boss, otherwise everything would be perfect.'

'I know.' Claudia adjusted her sunglasses on her nose. 'It's typical, isn't it? I finally meet the ultimate man, and I can't do anything about it. If it wasn't for David Stirling, I could be pulling out all the stops and maybe even *enjoying* being thirty!'

'You must be able to do something,' said Lucy, who hated the thought of Claudia missing out on such a promising relationship. 'You can't set out to seduce Justin while he thinks you're married to David—that wouldn't be fair to David *or* Justin, or Patrick, come to that—but perhaps when he sees that you're not going to do anything stupid you could ask David to tell Justin the truth?'

Claudia thought that she would rather die than beg David to do anything of the kind, but she murmured a noncommittal reply. Fortunately, Fiona and her mother arrived at the poolside just then and she was able to distract Lucy by waving at them.

Fiona looked even fresher and prettier in the harsh desert daylight than she had the night before, and she was touchingly pleased to meet Claudia again. Her admiration was so obvious that Claudia felt a little guilty when she remembered how jealous she had been. Fiona might have that lovely bloom of youth, but it was evident that all she hankered after was Claudia's experience and poise. Youth is wasted on the young: Claudia recalled the old adage and smiled wryly.

It was hard not to unbend when Fiona was pelting her with eager questions about working in television. Claudia couldn't help feeling that the younger girl betrayed her age most in being so impressed by everything that she had to say. If Fiona had worked her way up from junior secretary as she had, she wouldn't think it was nearly so exciting, but in the meantime Claudia was reluctant to disillusion her about the hard reality that lay ahead. If you couldn't dream in your twenties, when could you?

They were still talking when Lucy looked up from her conversation with Fiona's mother and waved over their shoulders. 'Here they all are,' she said, sounding pleased. 'David, Patrick, John...oh, and Justin.' She winked at Claudia, whose heart had given a queer jerk at the mere sound of David's name. 'We don't often see *him* here at this time of day!'

Blushing faintly, Fiona swung round in her chair. It took all Claudia's will-power not to do the same, but she forced herself to sit coolly and wait for David to appear. Not that it made much difference. She could feel his presence as vividly as if she had been staring at him, and her spine tingled at his approach.

David saw the proud tilt of her head and he hesitated. Patrick gave Lucy a casual kiss as he sat down, and the obvious thing would be for him to do the same for Claudia. He had promised that he wouldn't kiss her again unless he was forced into it, he reminded himself, but he could hardly ignore her, could he?

He compromised by stroking her hair and letting his hand rest against the nape of her neck. 'All right?' he greeted her.

Every single one of Claudia's senses leapt breathlessly

at his touch, and her heart began to thud slowly and painfully against her ribs. 'How did your meeting go?' she asked, trying to sound as if she hadn't even noticed that his hand was warm and secure at her neck.

'Quite well—well enough to deserve lunch anyway,' he said. Absently, he let his thumb caress the soft skin below her ear.

'Of course, we all know why David's so anxious to confirm this contract now,' said John Phillips, coming up with a tray of drinks. He put it down on the table with a teasing glance at Claudia whom he had met and liked the night before. 'Word has it that he needs the money to keep his wife in sapphire and diamond rings!'

'Not to mention those six children,' Patrick put in blandly.

'And two honeymoons!' Justin chimed in.

They had obviously been giving David a hard time all morning. Claudia remembered her story about the six children a little guiltily. She remembered making up something about a ring, too, but *two honeymoons*? She glanced up at David for guidance, and he smiled enigmatically.

'It seems that everyone was rather confused to hear from you that we were going to the Seychelles and from me that we were going to Venice,' he said smoothly. 'I had to confess that we couldn't make up our minds between the two.'

Oh, dear, perhaps they should have prepared their story rather more thoroughly? Claudia could see them all waiting for her to make some comment. 'Well, Venice wasn't really going to be a *honeymoon*, was it?' she said. 'We just talked about going there for a long weekend.'

'I see you've got yourself a wife with expensive tastes,' Joan Phillips said, smiling indulgently.

'So I'm beginning to realise,' said David. 'I hope

you're not expecting a sapphire and diamond ring every day?' he added to Claudia.

'Just once a year.' She pretended to joke. 'It *was* my birthday.'

'What's it like?' asked Fiona eagerly.

'Oh, it's very simple,' said Claudia, forced to improvise at short notice. 'Just alternate sapphires and diamonds, but it's beautiful. Isn't it, David?' she couldn't resist adding.

'I was surprised to hear that he'd given you a ring,' said Fiona's mother unexpectedly. 'I'd assumed that because you don't wear a wedding ring you didn't like them.'

There was a frozen pause. David's fingers tightened at Claudia's neck and her own mind went hideously blank for a few seconds. Why hadn't they thought of an excuse to explain the absence of a wedding ring?

'Oh, no,' she said, quite easily after all. 'I love rings. I'm just not wearing my wedding ring because my finger came up in an allergic reaction the day after we got married, so I'm having it coated while we're away.'

Lucy looked at her with admiration at such a glib lie, and David squeezed her neck encouragingly. Then, realising that he was still standing there caressing her neck like a besotted fool, he removed his hand hastily and, afraid that he would be unable to stop touching her, he deliberately went to sit between Fiona and John Phillips. That left a space next to Claudia, and Justin had little choice but to pull up a chair there.

Hurt by David's apparent rejection, Claudia turned pointedly to Justin with a brilliant smile. She thought she surprised an angry expression in his eyes, but the next moment it was gone and he was returning her smile so charmingly that she decided she must have imagined it.

David and Fiona were talking in low voices, and

Claudia watched them out of the corner of her eye while managing to carry on an animated discussion with Justin. Obviously David wasn't interested in Fiona, she told herself. She wasn't *that* silly. Fiona might be pretty and just the sort of girl that David liked, but she was also nearly twenty years younger than him, and Claudia couldn't honestly say that she had seen the slightest sign of flirtation between them. It was just that David seemed to *like* Fiona in a way he didn't like her. Look at the way he smiled so approvingly at Fiona. He never smiled at *her* like that.

Suppressing a tiny sigh, Claudia pinned the bright smile back on her face and redoubled her efforts to entertain Justin. With any luck, David would notice Justin laughing and realise that someone found her fun, even if he didn't.

David was having some difficulty holding onto his temper. He had already endured a trying morning as a result of all the ridiculous stories Claudia had told last night, and the discovery of how reluctant he had been to take his hand away from her neck after his decision not to get involved had frayed his temper even further. Now she was sitting there, deliberately flirting with Justin, while he had to listen to Fiona going on about how wonderful his supposed wife was.

'She's so glamorous,' Fiona was enthusing, 'but such fun. She had us all in fits earlier on! And she couldn't have been nicer telling me about her job,' she burbled on. 'She even offered to show me round the company next time I'm in London!' She looked at David rather shyly. 'I think it's marvellous to see a couple who've both got really interesting jobs. Claudia's lucky that you're based in London, though. If you were working out here like...well, like Dad, for instance,' she said, although David had the impression that her father wasn't the first example she had in mind, 'she would have to give up her job, wouldn't she?'

'There certainly aren't many jobs in television in Telama'an,' said David, trying not to scowl at the way Justin and Claudia were laughing together. What was so damn funny anyway?

'I wish I could be like Claudia,' Fiona said wistfully. 'She's got such a strong personality and she's so confident and charming and...sort of *focused*.'

'She certainly knows what she wants,' said David, but the irony in his voice was lost on Fiona.

'I know, and that's so important if you want to be successful,' she told him earnestly. 'Claudia says that there's nothing wrong with ambition. She looks so beautiful, but she's quite down-to-earth really, isn't she? And so kind. A lot of people would have been bored stiff being pelted with questions about their job, but Claudia was really encouraging.'

David was getting tired of hearing about Claudia. She never wasted all that charm and kindness on him, he reflected sourly. He looked down at Fiona's open expression. She was a nice kid, natural and completely unspoilt, but no matter how hard she tried she would never have Claudia's dash or glitter. A good thing too, he told himself. 'You should never try to be like somebody else,' he told Fiona in a firm voice. 'We all love you as you are.'

His words fell into a momentary lull in the conversation round the table. 'Hear, hear,' said Patrick, and Justin nodded his head almost fiercely. Nobody showed any sign at all of misinterpreting his words, but Claudia's eyes still narrowed dangerously. He had no business implying that he loved Fiona! He was supposed to love *her*!

She simmered over lunch. Didn't anyone else notice how David made a point of sitting as far away from her as possible? He was the one who had made such a fuss about putting on a convincing performance in public, after all, and now he was treating her as if he couldn't even bear to be near her.

Well, if she really had been his wife, she would be too proud to show that she cared, wouldn't she? She wouldn't embarrass the company by telling David exactly what she thought of him, much as she might want to. No, she would pretend that she hadn't noticed and keep the party going and most probably not get any thanks for it!

For David, the lunch seemed to drag on interminably. He was very conscious of Claudia being the life and soul of the party at the other end of the table. Her hands gesticulated extravagantly and her laugh rang out and every now and then she would shake her hair away from her face in a shimmer of pale gold. She was showing off, he thought, glowering dourly down at his plate. He couldn't understand why the others all seemed to be enjoying her company so much. Look at them, laughing, encouraging her, thinking what fun she was!

Fun? Hah! David hacked viciously at his steak. He had had more fun ploughing through financial forecasts on a wet November afternoon.

At last it was over. David glanced at his watch, and got to his feet. 'It's time we were getting back,' he said, ignoring Patrick, John and Justin who all wore identical expressions. So what if they had hoped for another quarter of an hour before returning to work? He was the boss, wasn't he?

The three other men had obviously made the same calculation. Pushing back their chairs, they stood up. John patted his wife's shoulder, Patrick ruffled Lucy's hair, Justin smiled ruefully at Fiona and Claudia, although Claudia didn't notice. Her attention was fixed on

David, who showed every sign of walking off with a general 'goodbye'.

'Aren't you going to say goodbye to me, darling?' she asked provocatively, and, tipping back in her chair, she put her face up to him to be kissed.

David stilled. Across the table, his eyes met a challenging smoky blue gaze. 'Of course,' he said evenly, and walked round to put a hand on her shoulder. 'I'll see you later,' he said, and, bending his head, he dropped a brief kiss on her mouth.

Claudia had steeled herself not to respond. She had wanted to provoke him, to show him that this was just an amusing little game as far as she was concerned, but the fleeting touch of his lips sent a shock of electric excitement jolting through her so that she drew a sharp, gasping breath when David lifted his head.

She found herself looking straight into his eyes, which held an expression which she couldn't identify, and she hoped desperately that he couldn't see how shaken she was. It served her right, Claudia knew that. She had made him kiss her, and he had, and she couldn't complain if she didn't like the result.

Or if she did.

It was Claudia whose eyes dropped first. She swallowed. 'Goodbye,' she said huskily.

She was careful not to provoke him again. That brief, shattering kiss was never mentioned between them. David didn't mention it when he came back that evening, and Claudia, who had been unable to decide whether she should apologise or pretend that it had never happened, was shamefacedly relieved to follow his lead.

As the days passed, they both made an effort to touch each other as little as possible. Once the fact of their marriage had been accepted, it was easy enough to get through the day without spending very much time together at all. Confined to a spartan compound, the ex-

patriate community was expert at making its own amuse-
ments, and there was a party or a barbecue or a supper
every evening.

Occasionally, David would put out a hand to catch
hold of Claudia and steady her if she stumbled, and once
or twice she stepped back against him by mistake at a
party, but both would jerk away as if from fire, and they
would mutter a quick apology. Claudia never got used
to the frisson that shuddered down her spine if David's
fingers so much as grazed her skin, and for his part
David tried to keep as much distance between them as
possible.

It wasn't too bad in the evenings, when there were
plenty of people around to break the tension between the
two of them. They could relax in a crowd, and even
found themselves laughing together as long as they
didn't spoil things by making eye contact, but as soon
as they were alone they treated each other with a cool,
meticulous politeness that only emphasised the stretching silence between them. Every night they lay silently
apart in the big bed and tried not to think about how
close the other was, and how easy it would be to slide
across those few, empty inches.

The days were almost easy by contrast. David was
preoccupied with meetings, while Claudia was happy to
laze around the pool gossiping with Lucy. One day they
explored the souk, in the town, where the dark little
shops faced each other across narrow alleyways and the
air smelt musty and heavy with spices. She spent hours
poring over the heavy Arabian silver jewellery but in the
end bought herself one of the brass coffee pots that were
so typical of the region.

'Give it a rub and see if your own personal genie
appears,' said Lucy as they strolled along the street. She
glanced at her cousin. 'What would you wish for?'

What *would* she wish for? Unprompted, David's features sprang into her mind and Claudia stopped dead, looking down at the coffee pot in her hand. She felt as if she had walked unexpectedly into a wall. She didn't want *David*.

Lucy was looking at her in concern and from somewhere Claudia summoned a smile. 'I'd wish for Justin,' she said almost defiantly.

'Really?'

Claudia had been about to start walking again, but she stopped at the evident disbelief in her cousin's voice. 'Yes, *really*,' she said. 'What's wrong with that? I thought you liked Justin?'

'I do. I'm just not sure that you do—or, at least, not as much as you say you do, anyway.'

'What do you mean by that?'

Lucy hesitated. 'It's just that you've had much more opportunity to fall in love with David than with Justin.'

The ground seemed to drop away between Claudia's feet, and she found herself struggling with a most peculiar feeling of terror, panic and sheer rage. 'In love with David?' she exploded. 'You must be mad! There's no *question* of me falling in love with him. I don't even *like* the man!'

'All right!' Lucy held up her hands in mock surrender, but her eyes were bright with speculation. 'It was just a thought, something Patrick said to me the other night.'

'What does Patrick know about it?' said Claudia furiously.

'He just pointed out that there's a sort of crackling—that's what he called it, anyway—between you and David, and I know what he means.'

'*Crackling?* Don't be so ridiculous!'

'Maybe "crackling" isn't a very good word to describe it.' Lucy tried to placate her. 'It's just that sometimes you and David are on opposite sides of the room, but somehow you can tell that you're both aware of each other. It's as if there's a connection between you, like an electric current.'

'Wh-what absolute rubbish!' The suggestion that she might be in love with David had knocked Claudia sideways and she was stammering in her haste to deny the very idea. 'I didn't realise you and Patrick had such vivid imaginations, Lucy! There isn't anything between David and me, and there isn't going to be!' Her voice sounded high and strained, even to her own ears. 'I've had to keep up the pretence of being his wife because I don't want to get Patrick into trouble with his boss, but if it wasn't for that I wouldn't touch the man with the proverbial barge-pole!'

To Claudia's despair, instead of being convinced by her cousin's vehemence, Lucy was looking increasingly intrigued, and, in desperation, she changed tactic.

'Look, I'm sorry,' she said after a moment. 'I shouldn't have flown off the handle like that, but love is rather a sensitive subject at the moment. I haven't wanted to say anything because I know it started off as a bit of a joke, and anyway, there didn't seem to be much point, but...well, I've fallen for Justin in a big way. I'm just feeling ratty because it's obvious now that I'm never going to have a chance to be alone with him, and I'm going to have to go home without knowing how he might feel if things had been different.'

Appalled to realise how badly she had underestimated Claudia's feelings, Lucy hugged her cousin. 'I'm so sorry,' she said humbly. 'I had no idea you felt so strongly about Justin, but you can always come back again when David's not around. I'm sure you and Justin could get it together if he knew that you weren't really married.'

'Maybe,' said Claudia, but she wasn't thinking about Justin. Her mind was ringing with the idea of David not being around. She couldn't imagine being out here without him.

How different would things have been if she had caught a different plane that day and met Justin as Lucy had planned? Justin was a nice man. He was kind, caring and good company, and if she had any sense she *would* be in love with him. The trouble was that he didn't set her heart pounding whenever he walked into the room. He didn't make every nerve in her body tingle with his smile. He didn't make her bones melt whenever he touched her.

And David did.

Claudia's step faltered. Oh, God, *surely* she hadn't done anything as stupid as falling in love with David Stirling? She couldn't possibly be in love with a man who disapproved of her as much as he did.

Could she?

She tested the idea out gingerly. It certainly hadn't been like this when she had fallen in love with Michael. Then she had been swept away in a romantic fantasy, blind to Michael's faults and Michael's lies.

This time it was different. There was nothing romantic about David. He was cold and irritable, and all he cared about was getting his wretched contract signed. He certainly didn't care about *her*. Claudia had noticed every time he'd recoiled in distaste whenever they'd brushed against each other by mistake. He could hardly have made it plainer that he disliked and despised her.

Still clutching her coffee pot, Claudia walked blindly down the street. There was absolutely no reason for her to have fallen in love with David. Except that she felt safe whenever she was with him. Except that she couldn't bear the thought of life without him.

Except that she had.

CHAPTER NINE

ANOTHER evening, another party. This time it was a barbecue at the Phillips'. David sighed when Claudia reminded him. He was fed up with evenings spent watching Claudia across a crowded room. 'I could do with a night without socialising,' he said, venturing a glance at her. She seemed very quiet this evening. With any luck she wouldn't want to go either. 'Can't we just make an excuse—say you've got a headache or something—and stay here instead?'

Claudia hesitated, torn between longing to be near him and terror in case she gave herself away. She would never last a whole evening alone with him. David could be uncomfortably perceptive when he wanted to be, and he would be bound to spot that something was wrong. He'd only been back five minutes and already he'd cast her searching looks. Then what could she say? No, I'm not all right. I've just realised that I'm in love with you? She could picture David's look of horrified disgust even now.

'You stay,' she said instead. 'I don't mind going on my own.'

Probably desperate to get a chance to chat up Justin, David thought savagely. 'If you're so keen, we'll both go,' he said shortly.

It ended up as a miserable evening for both of them. David felt dour and disgruntled, and although he made a herculean effort to be pleasant when he got there, he knew that he wasn't good company—unlike Claudia who seemed to have got over her earlier lack of spirits and was once again on sparkling form.

146

He had no idea what it was costing Claudia to keep smiling. Her face felt brittle, her jaw rigid with effort, and all she wanted was to throw herself in David's arms and beg him not to let her go. As usual, he stood as far away from her as possible, but she was agonisingly conscious of him. Every time he moved or lifted a hand or turned his head, awareness flared through her.

She glanced over at him. He was looking grim and even more formidable than usual, and there were lines of strain around his eyes. He was tired, she thought, guiltily remembering how she had insisted on coming out. They could have been alone right now, listening to the water trickle quietly in the courtyard pool, enjoying the peace. David could have been stretched out along the sofa with his head in her lap, and she could have smoothed the tension from his face.

The longing to be there was so acute that Claudia felt it like a knife twisting in her heart and she actually flinched. Looking over as if casually, David caught her involuntary movement and he frowned. Claudia was behaving very strangely tonight.

'What about you and David, Claudia?'

'What about what?' she asked, not really listening. David was putting down his glass. He was coming over. Her heart began to thud against her ribs.

'You're miles away!' Justin laughed.

Now Joan Phillips had diverted him and looked as if she was threatening to embark on a long story. Claudia bit her lip and turned back to Justin. 'Sorry, what did you say?'

'I was just saying that it's my turn to repay some hospitality, and I thought I'd invite a party out for an evening picnic in the desert. You haven't been out to the desert yet, have you, Claudia?'

'No, I haven't,' she said vaguely. Her spine was prickling...David must have made his escape from Joan.

Even as she quivered with awareness, David's cool voice spoke from behind her. 'Haven't what?'

'Claudia hasn't seen anything of the desert,' said Justin. 'I was suggesting a picnic tomorrow evening. We could go out to the wadi and watch the sun set,' he went on enthusiastically. 'You'd like that, wouldn't you, Claudia?'

Claudia felt David's eyes on her. Perversely, now that he was here, she wanted to drive him away. She couldn't concentrate with him standing there, just *looking* like that. She beamed at Justin. 'I'd love to. I've been longing to see something of the real desert. All I've seen so far is the road between here and Telama'an, and I'm sure there must be more to the desert than a dusty road.'

'There sure is,' grinned Justin. 'So you'll come along tomorrow evening?'

'Wonderful,' said Claudia, but David forestalled any further raptures.

'I'm afraid Claudia and I won't be able to make it tomorrow. We've had a special invitation to dine with the sheikh, so obviously that must take precedence.'

'We'll arrange another date, then,' said Justin easily.

'No, you all go,' said David, just as easily but with a certain steeliness that effectively dissuaded the younger man from insisting. 'Claudia will have other opportunities to see the desert.'

'Are we really having dinner with the sheikh tomorrow evening?' Claudia asked as they drove home.

'Of course.' David cast her a sardonic look. 'Did you think it was just an excuse for me to get you on your own?'

'No,' she said dully, wishing that it had been true. 'No, I didn't think that.'

Claudia leant towards the dressing table mirror and pulled the top off her lipstick. Behind her, David had just come out of the bathroom bare-chested, and he was rifling through the wardrobe for a clean shirt. She stilled, watching his reflection, the lipstick forgotten in her hand. His body was sleek and powerful and the memory of how it felt beat an insistent tattoo of desire over her skin.

Pulling out a shirt with a grunt of satisfaction, David shrugged it on and sat down on the edge of the bed with it still unfastened as he rested one ankle after the other on his knee and slipped on his shoes. Claudia knew that he was thinking about the dinner to come. Sheikh Saïd had been very evasive in meetings so far, and David was hoping that the dinner would be a good chance to persuade him to sign the contract at last.

Her eyes rested on his face as he began to button up his shirt, unaware of her gaze. She was desperately aware of time running out. In five days she was due to fly back to London and she would never see him again, and she stared at him almost fiercely, as if trying to imprint his features on her memory.

David was muttering over a recalcitrant cuff. He hoped Claudia wasn't going to be too long getting ready. They mustn't be late. Looking up to ask her how much longer she needed, he saw her watching him in the mirror with her great, smoky eyes, and the words died on his lips as the very air seemed to evaporate between them.

He forgot about the time, about the sheikh, about how important this dinner might be for the future of his firm. Nothing mattered but the tightness in his chest, and Claudia's eyes riveted on his, those eyes that could sparkle or glitter or soften with dreams or—like now—reach deep inside him and squeeze his heart until he was dizzy with wanting her.

Somehow David managed to jerk his eyes away. 'Are you nearly ready?' he asked. He sounded as if he had just run a marathon, and he felt like it as he stood up on ridiculously unsteady legs and concentrated fiercely on pushing his shirt into his trousers.

'Almost.' Claudia lifted the lipstick to her mouth, but her hand was shaking so much that she had to draw a deep breath and try again. The final result was distinctly wavery, but she blotted it with a tissue and hoped that David wouldn't notice.

Why should he, after all? He was knotting his tie, and his face was set in typically formidable lines. His mind was on the dinner and if he looked at her it was probably only in despair that he was saddled with an unpredictable companion on such an important occasion. She wouldn't let him down, though, Claudia vowed. It was the one thing she could do for him.

She turned to face him, lifting her arms away from her sides for inspection. 'This is my good-girl dress,' she said. 'Do I look modest enough for the sheikh?'

David let himself look at her. She was wearing a plain black dress which fell in soft folds beneath her knees. It had three quarter length sleeves, and a wide but modest neckline that threw the achingly pure line of her clavicle into relief. In spite—or perhaps because—of its severity, it was a subtly sexy dress. David wanted to walk over and jerk Claudia into his arms. He wanted to peel the dress off her and let it fall unheeded into a puddle of material on the floor. He wanted to carry her over to the wide bed and make love to her.

Instead, he cleared his throat. 'You look…very… suitable,' he said.

Suitable? Was that all he could say? Claudia fought down bitter disappointment. 'Good,' she said with a bright, brittle smile. 'Shall we go, then?'

David had warned her that Sheikh Saïd could be a difficult man to deal with, but Claudia found him charming. It was soon obvious that the feeling was mutual. David watched in amazement as the sheikh, normally irascible and formal to the point of rigidity, unbent in the face of her interested questions about his country.

It was a side of Claudia that he hadn't seen before. He had half expected her to show off, or alienate the sheikh with her sharp tongue, but she did neither of those things. Instead she was warm but demure, charming without being cloying, intelligent without being intimidating.

Initially wary, David soon realised that Claudia was more than capable of dealing with the sheikh without any help from him, and he allowed himself to relax. Sheikh Saïd was clearly much taken with her, and David himself was content to find himself sidelined in the conversation. He sat opposite Claudia and found himself noticing how her lashes tilted when she smiled. He watched the expressions sweep across her vivid face as she listened, saw how her whole body became animated when she talked.

There seemed to be so many different Claudias. Snappy, sarcastic Claudia; frivolous, flirtatious Claudia; dreamy, desirable Claudia; glamorous Claudia, funny Claudia, kind Claudia…and now Claudia the perfect guest who was behaving with model propriety.

How many other Claudias were there? Ever since Alix had left, David had avoided smart, sophisticated girls like her. Clever Alix, who had wreaked such havoc in his heart… It was odd, but for the first time in years he could think of her without bitterness. She had taught him a lesson, though, and he had stuck to girls with sweeter natures since then. Nice girls every one, and he had remained on good terms with all of them, but not one had tempted him to marry. Could it be because they had all been undeniably pretty, unquestionably nice but—just maybe—a little dull?

David's eyes rested on Claudia's vivid face. She was

exasperating, infuriating, unpredictable, restless...but never dull.

No, never, ever dull.

He was jerked awake by a sharp kick on his ankle. 'Sheikh Saïd was wondering whether you were going to have a chance to show me anything of Shofrar,' said Claudia with a minatory look.

'I do believe that he was thinking of something quite different,' said the sheikh, and David noted with relief that he had chosen to be amused rather than offended by his abstraction.

'I do apologise,' he began, but the sheikh waved a deprecating hand.

'Do not apologise! We must all make allowances for a man so much in love with his bride!'

For a fleeting instant, David's eyes met Claudia's, and then they both looked away. 'I congratulate you on your charming wife,' Sheikh Saïd went on. 'I have heard much of her, from my nephew, of course, but also from others in the town.' He turned courteously to Claudia. 'I understand that you bought a coffee pot in the souk the other day.'

Claudia's jaw dropped, and he laughed, gratified by her surprise. 'I have many sources of information, Mrs Stirling, and I know everything that goes on in my town.'

He didn't know that she wasn't really Mrs Stirling, though. 'I'm impressed,' she said weakly.

The sheikh snapped his fingers, and a servant materialised from the shadows with a box. 'I would like to offer your wife a gift on your marriage,' the sheikh said to David. 'I hope this will be a more fitting memento of Telama'an than a coffee pot.' He nodded to the servant, who placed the box in front of Claudia.

She opened it carefully. Inside lay a traditional Shofrani necklace, elaborately wrought in heavy Arabian silver and set with ruby-red stones that gleamed in the light. Intricately linked silver beads and balls dangled from it, chinking together as Claudia slowly lifted the necklace from its box. 'Oh, it's beautiful!' she breathed. 'I looked at some necklaces like these in the souk, but none of them were as magnificent as this!'

Sheikh Saïd was clearly pleased with her reaction. He pointed to what looked like a little cylinder pendant, decorated in delicate filigree work, that hung among the beads. 'That is a *hirz*,' he told her. 'A charm case. Open it.'

Claudia eased open one end and drew out a tiny piece of paper. 'It's in Arabic,' she said. 'What does it say?'

'It wishes you much happiness and many children in your marriage.' The sheikh beamed, and Claudia's throat tightened. He wasn't to know that there was no marriage, no happiness and no prospect of any children. Her eyes glimmered with tears.

'Thank you,' she said. It was all she could manage, but the sheikh seemed to think she had said enough.

'It's very generous of you,' said David as Claudia fastened the necklace and settled it against her throat, where it looked fantastically dramatic against the plain black of her dress and the luminous glow of her skin. 'It is a beautiful necklace.'

'A beautiful necklace for a beautiful woman,' said the sheikh gracefully, and David looked across at Claudia who was touching the beads with delight.

'Yes,' he said, but so softly that she didn't hear.

'You'll have to return it when I've gone,' burst out Claudia as soon as they got back to the guest quarters. 'I knew I couldn't refuse it, but it feels all wrong to be accepting such a present from him when all we've done is lie to him.'

'It's not very comfortable, I agree,' said David,

wrenching his tie loose. 'But he'd be more offended if we gave it back.'

'I suppose so.' She walked edgily over to the mirror and reached behind her neck for the clasp. 'Will you look after it, then?'

'I think you should keep it,' he said. 'He gave it to you.'

'Only because he thought I was your wife.'

'Because he thought you were charming,' David corrected her. He walked over and put his hands on her shoulders so that he could look into her reflected eyes. 'You were wonderful this evening, Claudia. The least you deserve is a necklace.'

Claudia glowed beneath his hands, thrilled by his praise but stupidly shy. 'I didn't do anything,' she mumbled.

'I think you did. The sheikh liked you, and that could make all the difference to our getting the contract.' David suddenly became aware that his thumbs were rubbing instinctively against the nape of her neck and he snatched his hands away and thrust them firmly in his pockets. Stepping away from her, he cleared his throat. 'It may not sound very adequate but...thank you.'

'There's no need to thank me.' Claudia's senses were raging at his nearness. His thumbs had seared her skin, and it had taken everything not to close her eyes and lean back against him. She fumbled desperately with the clasp of the necklace. 'It was what we agreed, wasn't it?'

'Yes,' said David slowly, watching the back of her bent head and marvelling at how familiar it was to him already. Within a few days she had become so much part of his life that he found it hard to believe that he had ever been capable of calmly discussing their pretend marriage.

Conscious of his gaze but unable to meet his eyes,

Claudia concentrated on the necklace, but it was impossibly fiddly, and she gave an involuntary exclamation of frustration.

'Do you want a hand?' asked David.

'I can't undo the clasp,' she said stiffly, terrified in case he thought she was deliberately throwing herself at him.

'Let me have a go.' She stood rigidly as he brushed aside the golden hair and lifted the back of the necklace, but his fingers felt thick and unwieldy and he fumbled with the intricate clasp.

A quiver passed over the back of Claudia's neck. 'I enjoyed the evening, anyway,' she said with an attempt at lightness, hoping that he wouldn't notice. 'And I got my very own charm.'

'Do you think he knew about those six children you're planning to have?' David tried to joke in return, but it was an effort when every fibre of his being yearned to slide his hands over her shoulders and pull back into him so that he could kiss the side of her throat.

Claudia mustered a smile. 'I'm not sure if six children would really count as a blessing,' she said huskily.

'Perhaps you can settle for just the happiness,' David suggested, and her eyes lifted unwillingly to meet his in the mirror.

What happiness would there be for her without him? Claudia's heart cracked, and her eyes darkened with anguish. 'Perhaps,' she whispered, and when David finally managed to undo the clasp she fled to the bathroom before he could see the tears that threatened to spill down her cheeks.

'More meetings,' sighed Lucy when there was no sign of David or Patrick at lunch the next day. 'I wish the sheikh would make up his mind one way or the other.'

The men didn't appear until half past six, by which

time Lucy had begun to fret. 'I'm sure something's
wrong,' she kept saying. 'Patrick always rings if he's
going to be late.' When they did appear, they both
looked serious, and Claudia's heart sank as they hesitated just inside the door and exchanged meaningful
glances at the sight of the women's anxious faces.

Without quite realising what she was doing, Claudia
got to her feet. 'What is it?' asked Lucy urgently, and
then David and Patrick both gave in and grinned triumphantly.

'We've got it!' Patrick staggered as his wife threw
herself at him with a squeal of excitement. 'The sheikh
finally signed the contract this afternoon!'

'Oh, that's wonderful news!' Claudia's face lit up in
relief and in the rush of euphoria David found himself
sweeping her up into his arms and swinging her round.
Laughing, she hugged him back.

She felt so right in his arms that David's grip tightened and before he could help himself he had kissed the
warm, fragrant skin of her neck. The touch of his lips
sent an involuntary shudder of pleasure through Claudia.
David felt her quiver and, suddenly afraid that it had
been with distaste, he released her abruptly. 'Sorry,' he
apologised in an awkward undertone, feeling gauche and
clumsy as a schoolboy. 'I didn't mean to do that. It's all
the excitement—I got carried away.'

Take it lightly, Claudia warned herself, although she
was ready to weep when he dropped her so brutally back
to earth. It didn't mean anything. 'Don't mention it,' she
said with a bright smile. 'You've got to share good news
with someone, and at least I was handy!'

It was a hilarious evening. Word of the contract spread
like wildfire, and there was an impromptu party at the
club that went on until the early hours. Caught up in the
heady atmosphere of celebration and relief, Claudia kept
forgetting that the future of GKS Engineering meant

nothing to her, except in so far as it affected Patrick and Lucy. She had no share in the optimistic plans for the firm's progress, she made herself remember bleakly. When she boarded that plane back to the capital, and then on to London, she would be flying out of David's life.

The thought was too desolate for the evening, and Claudia pushed it aside. She would be realistic in the morning, she told herself. For now it was enough to see the strain vanished from David's face. He looked younger and more relaxed than she had ever seen him, and belatedly she realised how heavily the responsibility for the future of everyone here must have weighed on him. That they appreciated what he had done for them was obvious, too, and for the first time Claudia understood how important it had been to them all that the sheikh had had no opportunity to be offended by conflicting reports of David's marriage. At least it made her feel as if she had done her bit, even if it had been her fault that the story had arisen in the first place.

'You must be very pleased,' she said stiltedly to David when they finally made it back to the guest quarters much later that night. It had been such a cheerful, light-hearted evening and they had had no difficulty in talking to each other at the party, but now that they were alone conversation kept petering out into uncomfortable silences.

'I am.' David dropped into a chair and blew out a gusty breath. 'The contract means everything to the firm. We've been trying for so long to bring old Saïd up to scratch that I'd almost given up hope.' He looked at Claudia who was perched uneasily on the edge of the sofa and wondering if it would look too presumptuous if she settled cosily down for a chat. 'I'm sure he only made up his mind after meeting you. Patrick suggested

you should be given a permanent place on our negotiating team!'

She smiled to show that she knew that he was joking,
even while the idea of a permanent place anywhere near
him wrung her heart with longing. 'Will you be going
back to London now that the contract is signed?' she
asked, fiddling with her earrings, her eyes flickering
from the bowl of fruit to the cushion on the sofa, to the
huge brass lamp that cast a warm glow over the room,
to anywhere except David's face.

'No.' David was having just as much difficulty finding
something to look at. 'Now that we've got the go-ahead,
the work's only just beginning. I'll be here at least another ten days, possibly longer.'

'Aren't you going to give yourself a break?' asked
Claudia without thinking. She risked a glance at him.
'You look so tired.'

The wifely note in her voice made her wince but
David didn't seem to notice. He rested his head against
the chair-back, and looked at the ceiling with a faint
frown between his brows. Weariness swept over him and
for the first time in his life he was conscious of a feeling
that might almost have been loneliness.

'I could certainly do with a rest from all this socialising,' he confessed. Lifting his head again, he looked
straight at Claudia and found her watching him from
under her lashes. Her gaze slid quickly away, faint colour tingeing her cheeks. He cleared his throat. 'As a
matter of fact,' he said hesitantly, 'I was thinking of
taking off to the desert tomorrow for a night of peace
and quiet. Do you want to come with me?' He had meant
to keep his voice elaborately casual, but instead it came
out in a rush.

Claudia swallowed. 'Wouldn't you rather be on your
own?' she made herself ask, even as every sense urged
her to accept before he changed his mind.

'I don't want to turn it into another party, that's all.'
David was taken aback at how badly he wanted her to
come. 'You said you wanted to see the desert, and it
might be your last chance before you go.'

Before you go. The reminder made Claudia pause. It
was madness to let herself get any more involved.
Wouldn't it be wiser to stay with Lucy and accept the
fact that she would have to live the rest of her life without him? She would have to get used to it sooner or
later.

David saw her hesitation and disappointment gripped
his throat like an iron fist, but he tried to be fair. After
last night, she didn't owe him anything. He was convinced that it was Claudia who had finally persuaded the
sheikh in their favour, and tomorrow night might be her
one chance to get to know Justin Darke as she wanted
without him cramping her style.

'Of course, I quite understand if you'd rather spend
some time with Justin,' he said in a colourless voice.

'No!' said Claudia quickly, overcome by panic at the
thought that he might leave her behind after all. 'I mean,
it would look a bit odd if you went off without me,
wouldn't it?'

'Yes, I suppose it would,' said David, hardly able to
conceal his relief at having a good reason for taking her.
'Well, if you don't mind...'

'No, I don't mind.' She drew a long breath of mingled
relief and anticipation. 'I'd like to come.'

Claudia was unprepared for the desert. She didn't know
what to expect—perhaps an extension of the flat, rubbly
plain that stretched interminably on either side of the
road between Telama'an and the site—but was too shiv-
ery with excitement to give it much thought.

When David picked her up, she felt as nervous and
exhilarated and shy as a schoolgirl on her first date. He

had arranged everything. Two mattresses were rolled up in the back, and he had borrowed sleeping bags and somehow talked the sheikh's cooks into providing a picnic supper. All Claudia had to do was step into the car as he held the door open with a flourish.

The afternoon glare faded out of the sky as they drove across the plain, and by the time the Jeep bumped to a halt the air was suffused with the golden light of evening. They were parked on the edge of a *wadi*, a watercourse gouged out by flash desert floods that left the ground to either side tumbled with rocks and boulders, eroded by sand and wind and age into weird and wonderful shapes.

Claudia felt as if she was sitting on the edge of the world. It was utterly quiet. The emptiness stretched out to the horizon around them. No cars, no people, no animals, no nothing. Just her and David. The glow of the sinking sun enveloped her in its unearthly light, and all at once everything that had seemed desperate and confused became very clear and very simple. 'I think,' she said slowly, 'that it was worth coming to Shofrar just for this.'

David sat on the other end of the mattress, keeping a careful distance between them. 'Even if Justin doesn't come up to scratch?' he asked, trying to keep his voice light.

Claudia turned to look at him directly. 'I'm not interested in Justin, David. I never was.'

'What about the famous prediction?' he asked suspiciously. 'I thought that was why you came?'

'I came because my life was falling apart and I needed somewhere to go,' she said. She looked back at the sunset. 'I never believed in that stupid prediction. Even at fourteen I knew better than to think that someone dressed up in a funny costume could see my future in a crystal ball.'

'Why did you say that you did?'

She shrugged, a little shamefaced. 'Just to annoy you really. It was childish, I know, but you seemed to disapprove of me so much and I couldn't explain the real reason I was so desperate to get to Lucy's in time for my birthday.'

'Lucy said that you had been engaged,' said David quietly.

'To Michael.' Claudia scooped up a handful of sand, let it trickle slowly through her fingers. 'It was all going to be perfect. I really thought that *he* was my destiny,' she went on with a twisted smile, 'but he didn't think that I was his. He came back one day and told me that he'd fallen in love with someone else. He said that I was strong and that I didn't need anyone to look after me like she did.

'Maybe I don't,' she continued, scooping up more sand, 'but it didn't feel like it at the time. There I was, facing thirty, and it seemed like I had lost everything I'd ever wanted. I was dreading my birthday until Lucy rang and persuaded me to come out here instead. As far as I was concerned, turning thirty was the end of the world. I'd had such a good time in my twenties, and I think I thought I was going to wake up on August eleventh middle-aged, with half my life over.'

Claudia looked down at the pile of soft sand beside her, and then at David. 'I woke up with you instead,' she said.

There was an airless silence while the memory of the kiss they had shared that morning reverberated around them. It was David who looked away first. 'I'm afraid I wasn't the most sympathetic person to spend your birthday with,' he said after a moment.

'You were what I needed. You made me angry, and I didn't care what you thought about me as long as you didn't feel sorry for me.'

David smiled. 'I've felt a lot of things for you over the last two weeks, Claudia, but I think I can safely say that I've never felt sorry for you!'

'I felt sorry for myself when that engine failed,' Claudia confessed, returning his smile almost shyly. 'I thought that life was trying to tell me something, and I wished I'd just stayed at home and been miserable and safe, but now...' She leant back on her hands and lifted her face to the sky, feeling the space and the light and the silence seep into her.

'Now?' David prompted, and she turned once more to meet his steady gaze.

'Now I'm glad I did,' she finished simply.

He reached out and picked up her hand almost thoughtfully. 'I'm glad you did, too,' he said.

The air evaporated from Claudia's lungs. 'Really?' she whispered.

'Really,' he confirmed. 'Are you really not interested in Justin Darke?'

A smile trembled on her lips. 'Really.'

David turned over her hand and pressed a warm kiss into her palm. Delicious sensations shivered up Claudia's arm only to snarl in a knot of quivering anticipation deep inside her.

'Really?' he teased softly, moving his lips to the pulse at her wrist.

'Yes,' said Claudia on a gasp.

She curled her fingers against his cheek, hardly daring to believe that she could touch him at last. 'Yes,' she breathed again. Her fingers spread tentatively, loving the male-rough feel of his skin, tracing the line of his jaw, drifting down the warm, strong column of his throat.

Without haste, her gaze lifted to meet David's, and for a long moment they simply looked at each other while a wordless conversation took place between them until, at exactly the same moment, they smiled slowly.

Nothing had to be said, nothing explained, nothing excused.

Claudia felt light, boneless with desire and drenched in the sudden, glorious certainty that everything would be all right. She was adrift in another world where nothing existed but the two of them and this spilling happiness, and everything was happening with a dreamlike slowness. She never knew whether David pulled her towards him or if it was she who leant into him, but at last, at last, she was in his arms.

When their lips met it was not with the suppressed passion they had known before, but with a wonderful sense of coming home. Claudia felt as if she had been pushed out on a swing into the sunshine. There was soaring delight and flooding warmth and wild exhilaration, and she slid her arms around David's neck and sank into his kiss, kissing him back as it seemed as if she had been longing to do for so long.

David drew her down onto the mattress, and she melted against him, her body warm and pliant and responsive. He couldn't hold her close enough as he kissed her hungrily and his hands moved insistently over her slenderness. Claudia's arms were round him, tugging his shirt free from his trousers so that she could spread her fingers over the firm muscles of his back and feel them flex at her touch.

The passion that had simmered between them for so long had exploded into a starburst of sensation that neither of them could control. Neither wanted to as their kisses grew deeper and urgent, their hands more demanding.

'Claudia...' David took her face tenderly between his hands. Claudia had never dreamt that his eyes could be so warm, and when she smiled lovingly up at him he caught his breath with desire. 'I've wanted to kiss you like this night after night,' he said, his voice ragged with passion.

'I don't believe you,' she managed breathlessly, thinking of those long, desperate nights when they had lain with those few inches like an abyss between them.

'It's true.' He kissed her throat, buried his face in her neck and breathed in the fragrance of her skin that had tantalised him for days now. 'I think I've wanted to kiss you ever since you sat down next to me on that damned plane and I smelt your perfume. Your hair was like spun gold in the sunlight. I wanted to run my fingers through it and feel whether your skin was as soft as it looked.'

Claudia stretched provocatively beneath him. 'But I thought I was the most exasperating woman you had ever met?' she teased, and shivered with pleasure as she felt him smile against her skin.

'You were, you are,' said David. 'It didn't stop me wanting you.'

'I wish I'd known,' she sighed. 'We needn't have wasted that lovely big bed.'

'This mattress will do as well,' he murmured, his fingers deftly unfastening the buttons on her shirt, and his lips following, trailing fire. When he pushed the soft material aside and found her breasts with his mouth, Claudia gasped at the silvery shock of sensation, and she arched towards him pleadingly as his hand slid lower.

'*David*,' she cried, reaching for him with a kind of desperation, but he captured her hands with a smile.

'Gently,' he murmured. 'There's no hurry. No phone is going to ring, no one's going to knock at the door. There's just you and me and a whole night to ourselves.'

He undressed her with a tantalising, excruciating lack of haste, savouring the texture and the taste of her skin as he went, while Claudia's bones liquefied beneath the blissful assault on her senses. She had never known such an intensity of feeling before, and she writhed, incoherent with desire, able only to gasp his name in a mixture of impatience and panic as she felt the last shreds of control slipping away.

David rejoiced in the knowledge that her need was as great as his own. He had discarded his own clothes and now treasured every tiny curve of her body, sweeping his hand up the smooth length of her thigh, kissing his way deliciously over the satiny stomach, unlocking her secret places with his mouth, questing, coaxing, loving her warmth and her fire.

Dizzy with excitement, her body thrumming, craving what only he could give her, Claudia rolled him beneath her. 'It's my turn now,' she said breathlessly, glorying in his unyielding strength. He was sleek and hard, and his body gleamed in the sun's last red blaze of light. His muscles were taut, like tempered steel, but his skin was warm and supple and her lips whispered enticingly over him, tasting him with her tongue, touching, tantalising until David could bear it no longer and swung her roughly beneath him once more.

'I thought there was no hurry?' teased Claudia, her fingers drifting wickedly down over his stomach.

'There is now,' said David, and then there were no more words. There was just the fevered heat beating through them and an instinctive, unstoppable need that swamped all else.

Claudia lifted herself to him, letting out a long breath of exquisite relief when she felt him inside her, and for a timeless moment they paused, looking deep into each other's eyes, before the need pushed them impatiently on, and they were rising, surging, clinging together as searing sensation swept them on and on in a wild, exhilarating rhythm that sent them plunging off the edge of the world together and shattering at last into inexpressible joy with a hoarse cry of release.

CHAPTER TEN

'MY FLIGHT leaves the day after tomorrow,' said Claudia inconsequentially.

The car was bowling along the ridged track that stretched out to where a shimmering smudge floating above the horizon marked Telama'an. Claudia wished they could go slower. She didn't want to go back. She wanted to stay by the *wadi* where the silence settled around her like a blessing, where there were no demands and no hassles and no image to keep up, where there was only David, like a sword between her and the rest of the world.

Holding him in her arms last night, she had discovered just how completely she loved him. They had eaten their picnic as the moon rose, and then they had lain on their backs and looked up at the stars. And later they had made love again, slowly and sweetly and so perfectly that Claudia had wept. Awed by the joy they had discovered together, they had held each other close, talking about nothing, just wanting to hear the other's voice and know that it was not a dream. There had been no one for miles around, but they had whispered, unwilling to shatter the magic of the still, dark night.

Claudia had fallen asleep at last in David's arms, waking only when the first rays of the sun tentatively touched her eyelids with gold. They hadn't spoken much then. They hadn't needed to, and after the wonder they had shared, what was there to say? David had made tea, and they'd drunk it sitting together on the mattress as they watched the sky turn blue. Then he had pulled her to her feet with a brief, hard kiss.

'It's time to go.'

Now the precious minutes were ticking away. Claudia hadn't meant to mention leaving, but somehow the words had come out.

'What, dare you get on a plane again?' David said lightly to cover his massive reaction at the thought of her going. She had sounded so casual, as if it didn't really matter, but her words had jarred him. He wasn't ready for them, hadn't wanted to think beyond the simple pleasure of having her beside him and remembering the night before.

'I'll have to,' said Claudia, disappointed and confused by his apparent lack of concern.

There was a pause. David gripped the steering wheel and stared straight ahead. 'Why don't you stay?' he said suddenly, as if the words had been forced out of him.

'I can't.' Claudia had noticed his hesitation, and the terrible suspicion that he might be only asking her because he felt that she expected it made her retreat slightly behind a mask of hurt pride.

'It was difficult enough to get time off from work as it was,' she tried to explain. 'It's all right for you. You own your own company, but the rest of us have to struggle to keep our jobs. I'd love to stay longer—I really would—but if I don't turn up on Monday there'll be somebody else more than willing to step into my shoes, and I can't risk giving up everything I've worked for just for a few more days.' She sighed wistfully and eyed the rapidly approaching town with dismay. 'I'm afraid we're on our way back to the real world now.'

David wanted to shout at her, to ask her whether last night hadn't been real, but he didn't. He remembered Alix packing her case. 'This is the real world, sweetie,' she had said. 'We've had a great time, but I'm not going to get on staying with you. I need someone with contacts, who understands how things work in the fashion world, someone who can help me.' She snapped her case closed with a small smile of satisfaction. 'And Tony has plenty of money, which also helps.'

He'd been young, he'd got over Alix, but it didn't make it any easier to sit and listen to Claudia talk about the real world too as if it was something separate, as if love was just an indulgence, an escape from the reality of work but not to be taken seriously in its own right.

Perhaps he wasn't being fair. She had a life of her own back in London. She had a job, a flat, family, friends. Of course that was more real to her than one night out in the desert, and he had no right asking her to give up any of it.

'I suppose you're right,' he said in a flat voice. 'The real world doesn't work like that, does it?'

Claudia sensed David's withdrawal and was hurt. He could have suggested that they meet up in London, couldn't he? Now she was reluctant to mention the idea herself in case he thought that she was pressurising him. What if he thought that she was going to pursue him as he had imagined her pursuing Justin, or that she was going to embarrass him by reading more into last night than he obviously had done?

They finished the journey in uneasy silence. When they got back, David showered and changed and went straight off to the office without even kissing her good-bye. He didn't trust himself not to catch her in his arms and beg her to stay, but Claudia saw only that he was brisk and businesslike and anxious to get back to the way things had been before.

They still had two nights together, Claudia reminded herself. She sat on the edge of the bed and memories of the night before shivered down her spine and soothed her sudden doubts. Tonight they would be alone again, and as soon as David took her in his arms everything would be all right.

*   *   *

'And I've got the most *wonderful* plan!'

'Oh, what's that?' said Claudia absently. Lucy had been chattering on as if they had been apart for months instead of just one night, but she hadn't been paying her much attention.

'Justin's going to drive you back to Menesset!' Lucy announced triumphantly.

'*What?*' Claudia was jerked rudely out of the dream where David strode in and announced that he had cancelled her ticket and refused to let her go.

'I've cancelled your ticket,' said Lucy.

For a moment, Claudia was utterly disorientated by this bizarre echo of her fantasy. 'You've done what?' she said in blank amazement, and her cousin leant forward.

'I've been thinking so much about what you said, and this just seemed the perfect opportunity to try and put things right.'

'What *I* said? What did I say?'

'You know, about never being alone with Justin or having a chance to discover whether he might feel the same way about you as you do about him. I felt terrible that I'd never even realised that you were in love with him, and I couldn't bear the thought of you going home feeling even more miserable than when you arrived,' Lucy explained. 'Then Justin said that he was driving up to Menesset tomorrow, and I thought if you could go with him you would have two days and a night to get to know each other properly at last.'

'Lucy—' Claudia began helplessly, but Lucy was still full of the arrangements she had made to make her beloved cousin happy.

'I told Justin that you were nervous about flying after what happened with the engine, and asked if there was any chance of him giving you a lift, and I must say, Claudia, he jumped at the idea! In fact, he was so keen that I'm sure he feels just the same about you. All you need to do is tell him that you're not really married, and I'm sure David won't mind if you're leaving anyway.' She laughed. 'It all seems to be working out so perfectly that I've even got myself believing in that prediction after all!'

'But—' Claudia broke off, looking at her cousin in dismay. Lucy had gone to so much trouble, she thought, remembering guiltily how she had tried to convince her that she was in love with Justin. This was her own fault. How could she explain now that she had only wanted to divert her cousin's suspicions from her own feelings about David?

She could tell Lucy the truth, but Claudia was strangely reluctant to say anything about last night. It had been too precious to be gossiped and exclaimed over, and anyway, she was still uncertain about just what it had meant to David. Last night she could have sworn that he loved her as she loved him, but he hadn't actually *said* so, and this morning he had been so distant.

No, she couldn't tell Lucy yet. She would have a quiet word with Justin and explain that she wouldn't be going with him after all, and then tomorrow she would book herself back on the flight. And tonight...tonight she would sort things out with David. Claudia's lips curved in a smile of sweet anticipation. Everything would be fine.

Later, she bitterly regretted not telling Lucy the truth there and then, but at the time it seemed easier just to smile and let her cousin burble on. Later, of course, it was too late.

They were at the club when David and Patrick appeared. There was no sign of Justin yet, and Claudia was sitting by the pool, gazing unseeingly at the water and wondering how long it would be before she could get David on her own. It was Lucy, on her way back from the loo, who spotted him as he came in, and promptly dragged him aside into the dining room, determined to spare Claudia the awkwardness of explaining the situation with Justin to him herself.

'David! Just the person I wanted to see! Listen, it doesn't make any difference to you if Claudia goes back tomorrow instead of Sunday, does it?'

Caught off-guard, David's heart gave a great lurch. '*Tomorrow?* Why?'

'Justin's driving up to Menesset and he can give her a lift.' Lucy lowered her voice confidentially. 'It's awkward for Claudia to tell you this herself, but she's fallen in love with Justin and this is their only chance to spend some time alone together.'

David could only think that there must have been some mistake. 'Are you sure that's what Claudia wants?' he asked and, as if in a nightmare, he saw Lucy nodding.

'Absolutely sure,' she said. 'Claudia doesn't usually talk about what she really feels, but she's been so miserable because she thought she would never know whether Justin might feel the same way. It's been really difficult for her wanting to be with him but having to pretend to be your wife.'

Lucy hesitated and looked pleadingly at David who was feeling as if he had been brutally thumped in the stomach. 'She's done everything you asked, David, and I know it was because she didn't want to make things awkward for Patrick, but you've got the contract now, and Claudia deserves a chance of happiness too. Let her tell Justin that she's not really married to you so that she can leave with him tomorrow. It's not as if you need her to be your wife any more, is it?'

'No,' said David, amazed that he could sound so calm when all he wanted to do was smash up every chair in the room and then beat the living daylights out of Justin Darke. Why hadn't Claudia said anything last night?

Had she really just been concerned in case he made things difficult for Patrick?

Claudia saw that something was wrong as soon as David appeared in the door. Her heart lifted at the sight of him, and she smiled as he and Lucy came across, but his eyes were blank and shuttered and he didn't smile back.

'I've told David that you're going with Justin tomorrow,' Lucy announced.

'Oh, but—' Claudia's eyes were stricken with dismay.

'At least you won't have to endure that flight again,' said David. His voice was light, pleasant, utterly controlled. The only way he could deal with the murderous rage he had felt when Lucy had broken the news was to seal it behind an icy numbness. 'It sounds a good idea to me.'

Claudia was shaken by the careful blankness in his expression. His eyes were quite unreadable, and, remembering how warm and loving he had been last night, she had the ghastly sensation that she was trapped in a nightmare. She even shook her head to wake herself up, but David was still there, looking cold and remote and utterly unreachable.

'You don't mind?' she asked in disbelief.

'Why should I? As Lucy has pointed out, I don't need you any more. Everyone knew that you were only going to be here for a couple of weeks, so they won't be surprised if you go a day early, and you deserve some time to yourself.' He turned to Lucy. 'Why doesn't Claudia spend her last night with you? It'll be much easier for Justin to pick her up tomorrow morning, and it doesn't matter as far as the sheikh is concerned. He knows she was due to go back early anyway.'

'That's a wonderful idea,' said Lucy enthusiastically, while Claudia could only stare at David. Why was he being like this? He wasn't even going to give her a chance to explain! Surely he knew that she would want to spend every last moment with him?

'What about my case?' she said in a painful voice.

'Perhaps Patrick would drive you over so you can pack?' David glanced at the other man who nodded and wisely kept his thoughts to himself. 'I want to go back to the office to wait for that fax from London.'

Claudia couldn't believe it. Was he really going back to his office to wait for a *fax* rather than be alone with her? Was he really going to walk off and leave her without so much as a flicker to show that last night had happened at all?

He *was*!

'I may as well say goodbye, then,' he was saying in that cool, polite, alien voice. 'Thank you for your help with the sheikh. No doubt you'll be glad to go back to being a single woman again.'

A welcome blaze of anger scorched through Claudia's numb sense of disbelief. How dared he make her love him and then treat her like a stranger? How dared he walk out of her life without listening to what she had to say? How *dared* he?

But then, if David really thought that she was the kind of woman who would sleep with a man one night and then promptly arrange to go off with another, she didn't want to be in love with him anyway! Let him go, let him walk off like the arrogant, pig-headed, *stupid* male that he was! She didn't care!

'Goodbye,' she said, with a tinkling, artificial laugh. 'It's been so interesting meeting you!'

For a second David's eyes flickered to hers and their gazes met, both hot, both bitter, both angry, and then he turned on his heel with a brief nod at Patrick and Lucy and strode back along the pool, into the clubhouse, out of her sight.

He was gone.

* * *

'Did Claudia get off all right?' David had pleaded pressure of work and refused all invitations for the last few days, but when Patrick dragged him almost forcibly along to the club he couldn't avoid Lucy any longer. He knew that he would have to mention Claudia some time, but her very name stuck in his throat, and his voice sounded hoarse and unfamiliar.

'I suppose so,' said Lucy glumly, wondering if he had a cold coming. 'She got to Menesset in good time for her flight, but the drive up wasn't quite what she had in mind. When Justin turned up to pick her up, he had Fiona Phillips sitting beside him, and poor old Claudia ended up playing gooseberry!' She sighed. 'Poor Claudia; nothing ever works out for her.'

David was furious with himself for the unthinking leap of his heart. He had spent the last days doing everything he could to erase all thought of Claudia from his mind, but nothing helped. It was like living with a ghost. Her perfume still clung to the sheets, and her presence shimmered in the air so that he kept turning round expecting to see her and then hating himself for being so bitterly disappointed when she wasn't there.

'Was...was Claudia very upset?' he asked Lucy, torturing himself.

'She didn't have a chance to say much, but I could see that she was trying not to cry,' said Lucy, who had practically been in tears of frustration herself. 'In fact, I don't think I've ever seen Claudia look so unhappy,' she went on miserably. 'It was awful. She was smiling and saying all the right things, but her eyes were just *desolate*. All she'd wanted was some time alone with Justin, and she didn't even get that.'

Claudia hadn't spent the night alone with Justin. It was all David could think about, and for a brief moment the cold claws that had been gripping his heart ever since she had gone eased their painful hold before settling back in with a vengeance. Lucy was the person who knew Claudia best, and if she thought that her cousin was really in love with Justin she must be right.

And Claudia hadn't known about Fiona when she'd cancelled her flight and decided to drive up to Menesset with Justin. She must have hoped to spend the time alone with him. If not, why hadn't she just refused? Why hadn't she simply told Lucy that she would rather stay with him?

Because she hadn't wanted to. David told himself it was time he faced up to the truth. What had he expected, anyway? That she would merrily throw up everything just to be with him? Real life wasn't like that, Claudia had said, and she was right. They had had a great night together—a wonderful night—but there had been no more to it than that.

It was his fault for falling in love with her when all his experience of Alix had warned him against it. Claudia just wasn't his kind of girl, and he wasn't her kind of man, and that was all there was to it. It was time to push the last two weeks into a mental box marked 'another painful lesson' and forget all about her.

It was no good. Claudia had done everything she could to banish David from her mind. She had thrown herself into work, volunteering for the most difficult tasks in the hope that when she got home she would be too tired to think, and when even the most tedious job had been done she dragged friends out to parties, to concerts, to the cinema, to the theatre, to anywhere where there was no opportunity to talk.

She couldn't explain about David. Claudia hardly understood herself why she loved him. All she knew was that at some deep, fundamental level he had become part of her and that without him she would never be complete.

It hadn't been like this when Michael had left. She had been hurt and miserable, but her self-esteem had suffered more than anything else. She hadn't felt this anguished sense of loss, this terrible emptiness, this feeling that every breath was a painful effort. David's image was always with her, and the memory of him made her bones ache with longing.

She couldn't go on like this, Claudia decided three ghastly weeks after she had flown back to London in a daze of misery. Maybe David *had* hurt her when he'd turned away from her so coldly that last day, but maybe he had had his reasons, and maybe—just maybe—he would change his mind if she abandoned her pride and told him how she felt about him. He might be appalled, he might be embarrassed, but if there was any chance at all that she could make things right, then she had to take it. Surely what she and David had discovered together under the stars was worth fighting for?

David would be back in London by now. All she had to do was ring and ask if she could come and see him. Claudia flipped through the telephone directory and then ran her finger down the page until it came to GKS Engineering Associates and stopped.

David was tired. He rubbed a hand over his face and tried to force his mind back to the proposal he was supposed to be drafting, but it was impossible to concentrate. It was September the seventeenth, his fortieth birthday, and never had his life seemed emptier or more bleak. Claudia would have said that he was having a crisis.

Claudia... The very thought of her wrenched at his heart. He had hoped that things would be easier once he got back to London where there were no memories of her, but the memories refused to be left behind in Shofrar. They came with him, lurking in hidden corners of his mind, ready to ambush him when he most wanted to forget, and now they were part of him: the tilt of her chin, the smokiness of her eyes, the intent expression as she put in her earrings.

Claudia had never been to his house, but still David found himself working late into the night at the office rather than go home and face the emptiness of life without her. He seemed to be getting wearier and more short-tempered every day, and his staff had learnt to treat him very warily.

Sighing David pushed the proposal aside and opened the top drawer of his desk. The necklace that Sheikh Saïd had given Claudia that night lay inside and he picked it up, turning the silver beads slowly between his fingers and remembering how she had looked as she'd fastened it round her neck. When he had eventually gone back to the guest quarters after leaving Claudia at the pool, it had been all that was left of her. She had packed her bags and gone, leaving the necklace on the dressing table.

David rubbed his thumb absently over the charm case and finally made up his mind. He couldn't go on like this. He had to see Claudia. He didn't know what he was going to say or what he was going to do, but he had to see her. Reaching for the phone, he punched in a number before he had a chance to change his mind.

'Patrick? David here.' He cleared his throat. 'Look, I'm sorry to ring you at home, but Claudia left a necklace behind in the room, and I thought she might want it back. I'd drop it off, but I haven't got her address...'

Claudia stood outside the GKS head office and looked up at the glittering glass façade with something like awe. Until that moment she hadn't realised quite how powerful David must be, and her nerve almost failed her.

Why would someone who had all of this waste his time with her?

Then she remembered how David had been under the desert stars. Neither of them had had anything there, had they? She had to trust that the man inside this prestigious building was the same man who had sat on a shabby mattress and made her tea.

If he was here.

Claudia had picked up the phone several times to ring him, and once had got as far as dialling the number, but each time she had panicked. What if she said the wrong thing? What if he was busy, or refused to listen? What if he listened but then said he didn't want to see her?

What if, what if...why didn't she just *go*? At least that way she would be able to see him. Anything would be better than just sitting there, wishing and wondering if things might be different.

Claudia drew a steadying breath and walked through the imposing doors into a light and airy atrium. Its gleaming modern lines were softened by cascades of plants and stepped pools of water that trickled restfully into each other. Claudia stopped at the sound of the water, overwhelmed by a sudden image of the courtyard at Telama'an, so strong that she could almost feel the cool tiles beneath her feet. If she closed her eyes she might be there, with David...

But David was here...she hoped. Stiffening her spine, Claudia walked over to a vast, curving reception desk and took a deep breath. 'I'd like to see David Stirling, please.'

'Have you got an appointment?' the receptionist asked pleasantly.

'No.' Claudia's heart sank. She had forgotten about the ranks of secretaries that the director of any firm like this would keep to stop any unwanted visitors. 'It...it's personal,' she said desperately.

'Just a moment, please.' The receptionist turned away and spoke on the phone, while Claudia stared blankly at the names of the senior personnel displayed by the lifts. It took a moment before her eyes focused on the name at the very top: D J Stirling, Chief Executive.

D *J*?

'I see that the initials J and D will be very important to you.' The fortune-teller's voice echoed eerily at the back of Claudia's mind, and a small shiver went down her spine. She hadn't said anything about what order the initials would appear, had she?

It didn't mean anything, of course, Claudia told herself. It was coincidence, that was all.

The receptionist was trying to attract her attention. 'I'm sorry,' she said sympathetically but very firmly. 'Mr Stirling can't see anybody at the moment. He's just on his way out.'

Claudia looked back at those two initials next to David's name. Maybe, just maybe, destiny was on her side after all. 'Could I speak to his secretary, please?' she said.

On the twelfth floor, David was shrugging himself into his jacket and telling Jan, his long-suffering secretary, to go home early when her phone rang again. She picked it up and listened for a moment. 'There's a Claudia Cook in Reception,' she told him, covering the receiver with her hand. 'She won't say what it's about but she says it's important. Do you want me to make her an appointment?'

'No.' David looked at his secretary without seeing her. 'No, tell her to come up.'

As if in a dream, he walked along the corridor to the lift. He watched the numbers light up one after another, bringing Claudia closer with every second, but when the lift sighed to a stop and the doors slid open with a soft ping he hardly dared to look in case she wasn't there.

But she was.

Claudia's heart was booming with nerves. She had been breathing very carefully—in, out, in, out—but when the doors opened and she found herself looking straight at David everything seemed to stop. Her heart paused in mid-boom, her lungs emptied of air and all she could do was stand there and stare.

David stared back at her as if expecting her to vanish. He had hungered to see those great smoky blue eyes again, had dreamt of the curve of her cheek and the line of her throat and the luminous glow of her skin, and now, suddenly, she was here and he couldn't think of a thing to say, could only drink in every detail of her presence and allow himself to believe that she was real.

Claudia never knew how long they stood there, just looking at each other. It seemed like a lifetime, but it couldn't have been all that long because the lift suddenly gave up waiting for another instruction and the doors began to close. Galvanised into action, David and Claudia leapt forward to stop them at the same time, and ended up in an undignified scramble, half in and half out of the lift before they realised how close they were to touching and immediately sprang apart again with embarrassed apologies.

Eventually, Claudia made it out into the corridor and made a heroic effort to calm her hammering heart. She swallowed. 'Your secretary said that you were going out. I'm sorry if you're busy. I...I won't keep you long.'

'It doesn't matter.' David got a grip on himself. 'Do you want to come along to my office?' That was better, he told himself. Cooler, calmer, less likely to terrify her then snatching her into his arms and refusing to let her go again the way he wanted to do.

They walked in awkward silence down the corridor. Jan was gathering together her coat and bag, and she looked up curiously when they came in. David looked

as if he had been pole-axed and the lovely girl beside
him didn't look in a much better state. Jan, who had
stoically borne the brunt of David's bad temper over the
last few days, looked from one to the other and drew
her own conclusions. She even managed not to smile as
David lost himself in the middle of an incoherent intro-
duction.

'Is it all right if I go now?' she asked.

'Yes, fine, absolutely,' said David, who hadn't taken
in a word. He held open the door to his office, and
Claudia walked past him on shaky legs.

Jan shook her head and smiled ruefully as they disappeared. It was a pity she hadn't asked for a pay rise
while she was at it!

David's office was huge and light, with windows
along two sides. Claudia went over and stood looking
out over London's pale grey skyline. She had practised
and practised what she would say, but now she was here
her mind had gone completely blank and all she wanted
to do was throw herself into David's arms and beg him
to hold her.

The silence seemed to gather force. 'I wasn't expecting to see you,' said David inadequately at last.

'No.'

God, she would have to do better than that. Claudia
drew a deep breath and turned round. 'I had to see you,'
she began. 'I've been doing a lot of thinking since I got
back from Shofrar.'

'What about?' he said when she seemed to stop.

'About destiny,' said Claudia with a half-smile, and
David stared at her, suddenly terribly afraid that she was
going to tell him about Justin.

'About *destiny*? I thought you didn't believe in it?' he
said bitterly.

'I didn't.' She paused. 'I still don't. Nobody can pre-
dict your destiny; I always knew that. Destiny is some-

thing you shape yourself. It's not something passive that just happens to you. I didn't meet my destiny when I was thirty...but I did meet you,' she added softly, and for the first time she could look at him directly.

'I don't think fate has decreed that we should be together, David,' she went on, gathering strength now that she had started. 'I don't know what life has in store. But I do know that my only chance of real happiness lies with you. I couldn't afford to leave that to destiny. I had to come and tell you myself.'

There was a long, heart-cracking silence. David was standing by his desk with such a strange expression on his face that Claudia was hit by the sudden terrible conviction that he was just trying to think of a kind way of telling her that she had wasted her time.

'You don't need to say anything,' she plunged on hastily. 'It was probably silly of me to come. I...I didn't want to embarrass you or anything. I just wanted to tell you that I love you.'

David still hadn't moved. 'It wasn't a good time,' Claudia stumbled on, edging for the door. 'I can see that now. You were on your way out, so I won't keep you any longer. I'll go...'

She was reaching blindly for the door handle before David spoke. 'Claudia?' he said quietly.

Claudia stopped, but she didn't turn round. 'Yes?' she whispered.

'Don't you want to know where I was going?'

David pulled a piece of paper from his jacket pocket and crossed to stand beside Claudia, who was staring at the door, rigid with misery.

He held the paper in front of her. Dully, she looked down at it, her eyes swimming with scalding tears, before a street name wavered into focus at last. 'That's my address,' she said uncomprehendingly.

'I asked Patrick to tell me where you lived,' said David. 'I was coming to see you.'

'Why?' she asked, still not daring to hope.

'I wanted to tell you that I couldn't bear living without you,' he said simply, and Claudia lifted her eyes slowly to meet his.

'Claudia...' David's voice shook as he reached for her at last.

'David,' she breathed. 'Oh, *David*.' And then his arms were around her and he was holding her against him with a sort of desperation, his face buried in her hair.

'I love you,' he said, kissing her almost frantically—her hair, her temple, her eyes. 'I love you, I love you, I love you.'

At last, at last, his lips found hers, and as they kissed Claudia felt joy spilling in a golden cascade along her veins. She wrapped her arms around David's neck and clung to him, half laughing and half crying between kisses. They couldn't hold each other tight enough, couldn't kiss each other deeply enough, couldn't hear often enough that the other loved them.

'I've missed you so much,' David mumbled into her hair some time later. He was sitting on one of the soft leather chairs set out for visitors and Claudia was on his lap, blizzarding tiny kisses over his throat. 'Don't ever leave me like that again.'

'Don't ever let me go,' she said, and his arms tightened.

'I won't.'

Claudia lifted her head and sat back slightly. 'Why didn't you say anything before I left?'

'Lucy told me that you wanted to be with Justin,' said David. 'I didn't want to believe it, but she was so sure, and suddenly...' He paused. 'I don't know...suddenly it seemed as if that night we'd had hadn't meant anything to you after all. I remembered what you'd said about returning to the real world, and I thought you were trying to find a tactful way to tell me that one night was enough as far as you were concerned.'

'But David, you know what that night was like,' Claudia objected, softening the effect by snuggling back against him. 'You must have known how much I loved you then.'

'I hoped you did,' he confessed. 'But I wasn't sure. I'm afraid that's Alix's fault.'

Claudia stiffened. 'Alix?' she said, with such an alarming lack of inflexion that David had to smile.

'I was engaged to Alix when I was twenty-four. She was very beautiful and very ambitious, but I was very young and I didn't realise just how far she was prepared to go to get what she wanted. That was, until I found out that she'd been sleeping with her boss on their business trips abroad and I learnt the hard way. When I confronted her, Alix seemed surprised that I was so upset. She accused me of not living in the real world, where you had to do whatever it took to get on. It didn't *mean* anything, she said.'

'Oh, David,' said Claudia helplessly, thinking how desperately hurt he must have been.

'Don't worry,' he said reassuringly, bringing her back against him. 'I got over her, but it did leave me with a legacy of distrust when it came to beautiful women and the real world.'

'Is that why you disliked me so much when we first met?' Claudia couldn't help asking.

David smoothed her hair lovingly away from her face. 'I didn't dislike you—I just tried to! But yes, you did remind me of Alix at first.'

'You don't think I'm like her now, though, do you?' she said, teasing feather-light kisses along his jaw.

'You're not like Alix, Claudia,' he said seriously. 'You never were. It was just that when you started talking about the real world, and then it seemed that you had leapt at the chance to go away with Justin...well, I was so jealous and miserable that I wasn't thinking straight. I haven't been thinking straight until today when I decided to come and get you anyway!'

Taking her face between his hands, he kissed her fiercely, and Claudia melted into him with a happy sigh. 'I still can't believe that you thought I was interested in Justin,' she said when she could breathe.

'Lucy didn't seem to have any doubts,' David excused himself. 'And she said that you looked desperate when Justin turned up with Fiona.'

'I only looked desperate because I'd spent the whole night breaking my heart over you,' she told him, and at last could laugh at the memory of that ghastly journey. 'When Lucy suggested that Justin give me a lift, he jumped at the idea because it meant that Fiona's parents would allow her to go as well. I was just along as a chaperon, but I wasn't a very good one because they were engaged by the time they got to Menesset!'

David laughed and tightened his arms around her. 'Do you know what the date is today, Claudia?'

She thought. 'The seventeenth?' Suddenly she sat up-right. 'September the seventeenth! It's your birthday!'

'My fortieth,' he agreed with a grin.

'Happy birthday,' she said, with a sweet kiss, and David smiled.

'It is now,' he said.

'So, what's it like being forty?'

'Wonderful! You should try it some time!'

Claudia leaned her cheek against his. 'Maybe in ten years' time. Until then I'm happy being thirty!' she said. 'Right now, it seems like the best time of my life.'

'There'll be even better times to come,' David promised, with another kiss.

'I haven't got a present for you,' Claudia mumbled happily when she emerged some time later.

'Say that you'll marry me,' said David. 'That's all I want.' He ran his fingers down Claudia's cheek and cupped her chin. 'You will marry me, won't you, Claudia, darling?'

'I think I should,' she said, pretending to consider. 'You might need to bid for another contract with the sheikh, and where would you be without me?'

'Talking of the sheikh...' David dug into his jacket pocket and produced the silver necklace that had been his excuse to see Claudia. 'Your first wedding present. You'll be able to wear it with a clear conscience now.'

'So I will.' Delighted, Claudia held it up so that the beads and balls chinked and chimed together. 'It looks as if his charm worked after all. Well, the bit about the much happiness, anyway,' she amended with a teasing kiss. 'We might have to work on six children!'

David smiled against her lips and tangled his fingers in the silky hair to pull her closer. 'We can start practising right now,' he said.

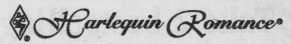

Harlequin Romance®

Everyone has special occasions in their life.
Maybe an engagement, a wedding, an anniversary, the
birth of a baby. Or even a personal milestone—a
thirtieth or fortieth birthday!

These are times of celebration and excitement,
and we're delighted to bring you
a special new series called...

One special occasion— that changes your life forever!

We'll be featuring one terrific book each month,
starting in May 1998...

May 1998—BABY IN A MILLION
by Rebecca Winters (#3503)
June 1998—BERESFORD'S BRIDE
by Margaret Way (#3507)
July 1998—BIRTHDAY BRIDE
by Jessica Hart (#3511)
August 1998—THE DIAMOND DAD
by Lucy Gordon (#3515)

Look in the back pages of any *Big Event* book to find
out how to receive a set of sparkling wineglasses.

Available wherever Harlequin books are sold.

Take 2 bestselling love stories FREE

Plus get a FREE surprise gift!

Special Limited-Time Offer

Mail to Harlequin Reader Service®

3010 Walden Avenue
P.O. Box 1867
Buffalo, N.Y. 14240-1867

YES! Please send me 2 free Harlequin Romance® novels and my free surprise gift. Then send me 6 brand-new novels every month, which I will receive months before they appear in bookstores. Bill me at the low price of $2.90 each plus 25¢ delivery and applicable sales tax if any*. That's the complete price, and a saving of over 10% off the cover prices—quite a bargain! I understand that accepting the books and gift places me under no obligation ever to buy any books. I can always return a shipment and cancel at any time. Even if I never buy another book from Harlequin, the 2 free books and the surprise gift are mine to keep forever.

116 HEN CH66

Name	(PLEASE PRINT)
Address	Apt. No.
City	State Zip

This offer is limited to one order per household and not valid to present Harlequin Romance® subscribers. *Terms and prices are subject to change without notice. Sales tax applicable in N.Y.

UROM-98

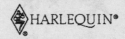

Not The Same Old Story!

Exciting, glamorous romance stories that take readers around the world.

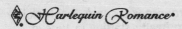
Sparkling, fresh and tender love stories that bring you pure romance.

Bold and adventurous—Temptation is strong women, bad boys, great sex!

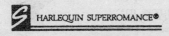
Provocative and realistic stories that celebrate life and love.

Contemporary fairy tales—where anything is possible and where dreams come true.

Heart-stopping, suspenseful adventures that combine the best of romance and mystery.

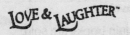
Humorous and romantic stories that capture the lighter side of love.

Remember the magic of the film
It's a Wonderful Life?
The warmth and tender emotion of
Truly, Madly, Deeply?
The feel-good humor of *Heaven Can Wait?*

Well, even if we can't promise you angels that look like Alan Rickman or Warren Beatty, starting in June in Harlequin Romance®, we can promise a brand-new miniseries: GUARDIAN ANGELS. Featuring all of your favorite ingredients for a perfect novel: great heroes, feisty heroines and a breathtaking romance—all with a celestial spin.

Look for Guardian Angels in:

June 1998: THE BOSS, THE BABY AND THE BRIDE (#3508)
by Day Leclaire

August 1998: HEAVENLY HUSBAND (#3516)
by Carolyn Greene

October 1998: A GROOM FOR GWEN (#3524)
by Jeanne Allan

December 1998: GABRIEL'S MISSION (#3532)
by Margaret Way

**Falling in love sometimes needs a little help
from above!**

Available wherever Harlequin books are sold.

The BIG Event

Toast the special events in your life with Harlequin Romance®!

With the purchase of *two* Harlequin Romance® BIG EVENT books, you can send for two sparkling plum-colored Wine Glasses, retail value $19.95!

To complete your set, see details inside any Harlequin Presents® title in September 1998!

ACT NOW TO COLLECT TWO FREE WINE GLASSES!

Fill in the official proof-of-purchase coupon below and send it, plus $2.99 U.S./$3.99 CAN. for postage and handling (check or money order—please do not send cash), to Harlequin Books: In the U.S.: 3010 Walden Avenue, P.O. Box 9077, Buffalo, NY 14269-9077; In Canada: P.O. Box 609, Fort Erie, Ontario L2A 5X3. Please allow 4-6 weeks for delivery. Order your set of wine glasses now! Quantities are limited. Offer for the Plum Wine Glasses expires December 31, 1998.

Harlequin Romance®—The Big Event!

OFFICIAL PROOF OF PURCHASE

"Please send me my TWO Wine Glasses"

Name: _____

Address: _____

City: _____

State/Prov.: _____ Zip/Postal Code: _____

Account Number: _____ 097 KGS CSA6 193-3

HRBEPOP

HARLEQUIN®
Makes any time special ™

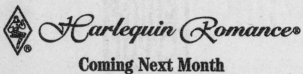

Harlequin Romance®

Coming Next Month

#3515 THE DIAMOND DAD Lucy Gordon
Garth had promised his wife diamonds for their tenth anniversary—
Faye didn't want diamonds, she wanted a divorce! But with two gorgeous
children and his beautiful wife at stake, Garth was determined to do all
he could to save his family!

The Big Event! *One special occasion—that changes your life forever.*

#3516 HEAVENLY HUSBAND Carolyn Greene
It seemed incredible, but when Kim's ex-fiancé Jerry woke from his
accident he seemed like a totally different man. Instead of a womanizing
workaholic, he'd become the perfect hero. He said she was in danger,
and that she needed his protection. But the only danger Kim could
foresee was that maybe heaven *was* missing an angel—and they'd want
him back!

Guardian Angels: *Falling in love sometimes needs a little help from
above!*

#3517 THE TROUBLE WITH TRENT! Jessica Steele
When Trent de Havilland waltzed into Alethea's life, she was already
wanting to leave home. So Trent's idea that she move in with him could
have been the ideal solution. But Alethea's trouble with Trent wasn't so
much that she was living with him, but that she was falling in love with
him!

Look out also for another great **Whirlwind Weddings** title:

#3518 THE MILLION-DOLLAR MARRIAGE Eva Rutland
Tony Costello only found out about his bride's fortune after their
whirlwind romance had ended in a trip to the altar. He couldn't forgive
her for being rich and for keeping it a secret. Melody had deliberately
tried to conceal her true worth for the sake of Tony's pride; now she
would have to fight to save their marriage. Rich or poor, she loved
Tony—she was just going to have to prove it!

Whirlwind Weddings: *who says you can't hurry love?*